FLORA NWAPA

NEVER AGAIN

AFRICA WORLD PRESS
TRENTON | LONDON | CAPE TOWN | NAIROBI | ADDIS ABABA | ASMARA | IBADAN | NEW DELHI

AFRICA WORLD PRESS
541 West Ingham Avenue | Suite B
Trenton, New Jersey 08638

First published in Nigeria by TANA PRESS, 1975

First Africa World Press edition 1992

Cover design and illustration: Ife Designs

Library of Congress Catalog Card Number:
ISBN: 0-86543-318-6 Cloth
        0-86543-319-4 Paper

ABOUT THE AUTHOR

Flora Nwapa is Nigeria's first woman novelist, author of the highly praised *Efuru, Idu, This is Lagos and Other Stories, Women are Different, Wives at War* and *One is Enough.*

For the mysterious and beautiful . . . Uhamiri

After fleeing from Enugu, Onitsha, Port Harcourt and Elele, I was thoroughly tired of life. Yet how tenaciously could one hold on to life when death was around the corner! Death was too near for comfort in Biafra. And for us who had known no danger of this kind before, it was hell on earth. I meant to live at all costs. I meant to see the end of the war. Dying was terrible. I wanted to live so that I could tell my friends on the other side what it meant to be at war – a civil war at that, a war that was to end all wars. I wanted to tell them that reading it in books was nothing at all; they just would not understand it. I understood it. I heard the deadly whine of shells. No books taught us this. And no teachers made us hear shells when they taught us about the numerous wars staged in Western Europe and America. But they couldn't have made us hear shelling. They had not heard it themselves. Their teachers had not heard it either.

When for two weeks in Port Harcourt we heard nothing but the angry booming of our gun-boat amidst a savage orchestra of exploding shells and rockets and the sound of small arms, I knew the game was up. I had told Chudi that Port Harcourt was in great danger, and would fall at any time. This was about two months before it actually fell. He was so upset that he threatened to hand me over to the Civil Defenders or the Militia. But I had never seen him so angry.

'If you think, woman, that we are going to leave Port Harcourt for the Vandals you are making a great mistake,' he roared. 'We will do no such thing. We will all die here rather than leave Port Harcourt.'

I laughed a mirthless laugh. Quietly, I said, 'Calabar fell ages ago. Calabar is forgotten. Port Harcourt will fall, and when it falls, it will be forgotten as well. This is Biafra. I have heard so much about Biafra. I did not hear so much about Nigeria when I was a Nigerian.'

My husband looked at me intently; without a word he opened the door and went out. Why talk to a mad woman? He hadn't fled yet.

We were separated when the war broke out and he had to go to Port Harcourt for an assignment given to him by his bank. I remained in Enugu, helping to organise the women.

The door opened after a few minutes and someone came in with my husband. He had not gone to call the Civil Defenders, I thought, almost collapsing. I managed to move forward and saw that it was our good friend Kal. Kal had been very strange of late. He was so pro-Biafra that I had begun to be scared of him. But he was not the type to take me to the Civil Defenders. He still had good sense in him. He sat down and I gave him something to drink. It was vodka. How strange. That was all I could get in the shop – vodka. Every other thing had gone. Vodka was not popular in this part of the world.

'Kal has good news,' my husband said.

In spite of all my frustrations, I listened. 'Good news. We hear good news every day,' I said under my breath. 'What is the good news?' I asked. 'Where is the enemy "bottled up" this time. In Aggrey Road?'

Kal was angry. It showed in his eyes. But he controlled his anger. Chudi made to say something, thought better of it and shut his mouth. Only his compressed lips and his eyes betrayed his anger.

Then Kal said. 'Kate! people like you should go into detention and remain there until the end of the war, and the State of Biafra fully established. You are too dangerous.'

2

He meant what he said. I was afraid, genuinely afraid. He believed in Biafra. I had believed too. But that was long ago. I remembered the day, Chudi had gone to Port Harcourt for the assignment. I was alone with the children, and Bee had come to see me. She had returned from Lagos and had not found a job yet, so she was threatening to go back to Lagos. Then Biafra was declared and she raced back to Lagos, then back to Enugu in confusion. Bee was there, and Kal was there. Kal was running after Bee then, though he was married. That day, long long ago Biafra was declared. We stood and heard our national anthem, and the speech. It was six in the morning. The anthem was inspiring. Everything then was inspiring.

The good news. Our gallant mercenary who was supposed dead was alive. We had just received sophisticated weapons from Europe. The name of the donor was top secret. 'But that was no news,' I thought, but I controlled myself. I had my children to look after so I didn't want to be detained. Kal meant every word he said.

Exactly two days after, my husband and I fled from Port Harcourt. He was the first to go, in an empty car for fear that he would not be allowed through the numerous check points. I took my five children and a few belongings in the big car.

On arrival at Ugwuta we told our people we were home for the week-end. We dared not tell them that Port Harcourt was under siege. We would be called saboteurs. That evening Kal came to see us. Kal returned before us? Wonders will never end in Biafra then, anything was possible. I asked my sister in-law when Kal had returned, and was told that he had returned on Thursday. The day my husband threatened to hand me over to the Civil Defenders. The day Kal came to us with the good news.

3

Chudi could not forget the experience of Port Harcourt. But for me he would have returned home with only the clothes he was wearing and his car. This was not going to happen to him again.

About five months later, our home was threatened. Ugwuta was threatened. It was not possible. How could that be? If Ugwuta could be threatened, then that was the end not only of the war, but of the world. It was just impossible. Absolutely impossible. The Woman of the Lake would not allow it. She had never allowed the conquest of Ugwuta by water or by land or by air.

To make sure that Ugwuta would not fall, the people, as early as the beginning of the war, had sacrificed a white ram to the Woman of the Lake. I was in Ugwuta then. The Dibia had come from far away. Nobody knew from where. Only the Divisional Officer and the army officer who brought him knew. It was kept top secret. People saw the Dibia on the Lake. That was no secret. He sacrificed to the Woman of the Lake and went away the same day. Rumour had it that he also sacrificed in the River Niger and in the creeks of Port Harcourt. These two places had fallen. But Ugwuta will not fall. I was sure of that. I kept on telling myself that Ugwuta will not fall; though I was afraid.

It was September and I was working. There was nothing to do actually. In the morning, when we came to work we went to look for something to eat. It took about two hours. Then we returned and talked of the war. On this occasion a girl civil defender mounted the rostrum. She had good news to tell us and we were very eager to listen. In spite of everything I wanted to hear good news. She was at the S&T that morning, and one of the officers had told her that Lagos and Ibadan were being shelled. Lagos had been shelled from the sea in the early hours of the morning, while Ibadan was being shelled from Lagos. Gowon had protested to one of the embassies, she did not know which one. As a matter of fact

4

Lagos was being evacuated.

Good news indeed. I knew Lagos very well. And I was angry. Why do they keep telling us this kind of story? Before we fled from Port Harcourt we had heard that our boys had made a bomb which could sink Lagos in under twenty four hours. They had wanted to use it, but our Military Governor, Ojukwu, had begged them not to. The boys could not be restrained any longer. In fact, they were now getting ready to use the bomb.

I returned from work one evening and Chudi said he'd tuned into the BBC. According to the radio station, Lagos was preparing an amphibious attack on Ugwuta, the gateway to the Uli airstrip. I developed diarrhoea immediately. I went to the toilet twice before I sat down to absorb the news quietly and reflect on the implications. I took it very seriously. I called my mother-in law and told her. She was angry. 'Are they coming tomorrow?' she asked.

'No, they said in two weeks. That is a long time, though not too long,' I said.

'Then please leave me in peace. They will not come. It is just empty talk. They cannot come by water. Never in the history of Ugwuta did an invader come by water and go home alive. So my mother told me. And nothing that my mother told me has yet been proved false. You are children. Trust in God. Trust in the Woman of the Lake. She has never let her people down. She is our goddess.'

I was not safisfied with this. To me God did not intervene in the affairs of Nigeria and Biafra. God had nothing at all to do with it. Not long ago in Nigeria we prayed to one God. Now we had two gods: The god of Nigeria and the god of Biafra. So I went to see my own mother. She listened to me and when I finished she told me there was no need to panic. All would be well, I seemed to forget that there was a God.

'Mama, not again,' I said.

'Wait, my daughter. I know we are getting old. But listen

to me first. You can do whatever you like to do after. But first of all listen to me. God is alive. God has been protecting us ever since we were born. And He will continue to protect us. We have been praying to Him and He can't give a deaf ear to our prayers . . .'

'But that is exactly what He has done. Please leave God alone. He has nothing to do with this. You said this in Onitsha when I told you that Enugu was threatened. You remained in Onitsha until the last day. You lost everything. What I am telling you, what I have come to tell you is to start making preparations for evacuation. We would like to be together and die together when death comes. If the Vandals meet us at home, none of us will be alive. And even if they are wiped out in under an hour we can never come back here again until the war ends. And when will it end?'

'I keep saying that you are not like me, Kate. You are not like your father either. Listen to me, God knows best. God has His way. We human beings want our will to be done, and not God's will. And . . .'

I was gone. There was no point at all in listening to Mama. This was not the time for preaching. But in the evening she was at our house, to see my mother-in-law. When they both came to our room, I was busy packing.

'When you are packing, shut the door,' my mother-in-law said. 'People talk a lot these days. When they see you packing they will say you are a saboteur.' I did not heed her. I went on packing.'

'I think we should start getting our things together', my mother said. 'Who wants to leave his home for the Nigerians? But if we are forced to leave, we shall have no alternative. I am going to start packing myself.' I could see that she took in what I said to her. I could see that her waist was bulging. She had wrapped her trinkets round her waist. And she was very worried indeed. My mother-in-law kept on saying that nothing would happen. And I was forced to talk.

6

'I am not praying that anything should happen. That the Vandals should invade us. Far from it. But if they do come, what are we going to do? You have to prepare yourself. We are all agreed that nobody should remain behind. And woe betide anybody who remains behind. When the time comes to run nobody will tell you. The time has not yet come.'

The next days were dominated by painful uncertainty. Chudi returned one day to say that all able bodied men had been asked to report at the school hall. And he was going. He did not like meetings, but he said he would go because he did not want to be misunderstood. I said I would go with him. So at the scheduled time we were at the school hall. To our disappointment, it was Kal who had called the meeting. There were a few men and women there as well. They were the old politicians. I did not like them. To my way of thinking they caused the war. And they were now in the forefront again directing the war. The women especially were very active, more active than the men in fact. They made uniforms for the soldiers, they cooked for the soldiers and gave expensive presents to the officers. And they organised the women who prayed every Wednesday for Biafra. In return for these services, they were rewarded with special war reports exclusive to them and them alone.

It was one of the prominent women who addressed the gathering of the men – mostly young men in their twenties and thirties. She was not quite forty years old and had four boys who were below fifteen years of age. Chudi did not like her at all because of a raw deal he had with her before the war. But she was so powerful then that people were very careful not to offend her. In short she was highly respected, feared, and hated. We had no alternative but to listen to her.

'My fellow Ugwuta people,' she started. 'A lot of people have been carrying false rumours. I am sorry for them. If

7

they are caught, not only will they be detained but their relations as well. I am for Biafra. I am for Ojukwu. I follow him wherever he leads. I have made this very clear. You all know me very well, though I have never lived at home. You all know that I lost my husband in this war ...'

'Why is she lying?' I said under my breath. 'Why should she lie with that kind of thing? Everybody here knows that her husband died a natural death in Warri in 1966. It was not a mysterious death either. He died in hospital of diabetes.'

Chudi glared at me warningly, and looked furtively about to see if I had been overheard.

'You all know that I lost all my property in Warri.'

'That's a lie again,' I said and earned a painful nudge from Chudi. It was annoying. The woman politician did not lose anything in Warri. When her husband died, she brought her children home, and her property. What she left behind was her landed property.

I heard her repeating the lie, 'You all know that I lost all my property in Warri. That is beside the point. What is property? I don't mind that at all. That is my sacrifice for Biafra, for the cause of Biafra. There is no sacrifice too great for Biafra. I am prepared to die for Biafra. My fellow Ugwuta men and women. We have fled from Enugu, Onitsha, and Port Harcourt. Where are we going to flee to again? Where are we running to? Why are we running? We are running from the Vandals. Who are the Vandals? Who are they? They are nobody. We must continue fighting against them until we vanquish them. God is alive and God knows that our cause is just. They killed us in Lagos, they killed us in Zaria, in Kano, in Jos, in Kafanchan, in Ibadan, in Abeokuta. We said to them, it is enough. Leave us alone in peace. We are going to our home. We will have nothing to do with you any more. You say we are land thirsty. All right. We are leaving your land for you. We are going back to our land. We shall work on our land. We shall keep alive. Live in peace in your Nigeria. You no longer want us in Nigeria. We are going back home. Then we called our home Biafra. *Biafra Kwenu Kwenu* Kwenu!' And the people responded with a thunderous '*Hee*' . . . . .

'My fellow Ugwuta people, the Nigerians will not leave us alone. The Vandals said we have committed a crime by leaving them. Can you imagine that, my fellow women here? Can you imagine it? If you are fighting and you are beaten and battered. You run home and lock your door, barring the man beating you. Then he turns round and says you have committed a crime. A crime, my people. Is cowardice a crime? We have agreed that we are cowards in Nigeria, not in Biafra. We shall defend every inch of our fatherland. God is on our side. We shall overcome. My people, we shall overcome. We shall overcome only when you men here stand fast and defend our land.

'Why am I a woman? God, you should have made me a man. I would have said to the young men, to the youths whose blood I know is boiling now in their veins, follow me. I'll lead you. I'll fight the Vandals. They will not be allowed to pollute our fatherland. They will not be allowed to set their ugly feet on the soil of Ugwuta. Never in history, my grandfathers and greatgrandfathers never told me that Ugwuta had suffered from any aggressor. This will not happen in my life time!'

'Woman, sit down, you have spoken enough,' one ruffian said. Everybody turned round to see the intruder. And he mounted the chair he was sitting on. Many people hissed as they saw him.

'Please push him out!' many said from the audience.

'Don't push him out. Hear what he is going to say,' others said. There was commotion. Somehow after a few minutes the hall was quiet again. It was not the woman who was talking now. It was the intruder. He had come up to say something.

He was very serious and rough. He had been militia in Port Harcourt. After the fall of Port Harcourt, he returned home following the new policy the government had adopted in making everybody a soldier, and scrapping militia men. He opted to return home rather than join the army. He had told everybody of the gruesome experience he and other militia men had as Port Harcourt fell. His relatives had begged him not to talk in the way he was talking, but he had refused. So they bundled him away to the farm. When the people seemed to have forgotten him, he emerged again.

'Look, you ruffian, you good for nothing child,' said one from the crowd, if you don't take time, if you are not careful, you are going to be handed over to the Army.'

'You can't hand him over to the Army,' another said. He was the uncle of the intruder.

'Allow him to speak, allow him to speak,' filled the hall.

'We have a chairman in this gathering. Ugwuta people, I am ashamed of you. I, the daughter of Ngenege, stood up to talk, and I was hushed down. I was hushed down. And I hear people saying, allow him to speak, allow him to speak. Allow who to speak? This ruffian, this intruder, this deserter? We should if we were loyal to our fatherland, Biafra, hand him over to the Army because he is a deserter. He is a good for nothing child. I wouldn't like to have such a child. God, please don't give me such a child . . .'

'No, no, no,' the Chairman said at last. 'I have given the intruder permission to speak. He should be heard, even if he is a deserter and a ruffian, he should be heard.'

'I don't mind what you call me in this gathering. I don't care at all. Everybody knows me here. Everybody knows my father and my mother. We are poor. But we are respectable. I was in Port Harcourt. I joined the Militia. And when it was time to fight, I fought for Biafra. We were cut off in the creeks. Many who could not swim perished in the creeks of Port Harcourt. Because I am from Ugwuta, the lake city, I

10

: to swim out, and to find my way home after hiding
ᴇeks for two weeks. It is because I am from Ugwuta
ı living now. Otherwise I would have been a dead
ow, and would have been forgotten as those friends
'ho were in the Militia with me, are now forgotten.
Ugwuta. I am concerned that harm might befall
'll fight with all my might to save Ugwuta from the

ınt to tell you something. Please don't say I am a
not. When the time comes to send away the
! the children, please don't hesitate to do so. The
young men can stay to defend Ugwuta. But please send the
women and children to safety. Don't leave them until the last
moment; if you do, many will die. This is the mistake that
was made in almost all the places that have fallen. This is my
home. I don't want it to fall. But please evacuate the women
and children first. Please . . .'
   'Let me answer him Chairman,' One of the men in the
audience said. 'When we evacuate the women and the
children, who will cook for the soldiers? Who will fetch
water for the women to cook for the soldiers? My people,
didn't I say that this boy is a *sabo*? We should hand him over
to the Army. I am a man and I am going to defend Ugwuta.
People like this boy should not be allowed to speak in a
meeting like this. Youths of this town should be ashamed of
themselves. I am ashamed of you, the Intruder (His name
was Adigwe, but the Intruder he was called from that day.) I
have two boys in the Army, thank God. I don't mind
sacrificing them for Biafra.'
   It was true he had two boys in the Army. One was a Major,
the other was a Captain. They had fought gloriously for the
cause. They were among the lucky ones who had survived
the war. I say, survived the war, because the rate of officer
casualties was almost criminal. Those boys fought so
bravely.

11

'That child is dangerous,' people shouted from the crowd. 'When the women and the children leave, who will cook for us?' many asked. 'Please let's go on with the meeting,' others shouted.

The Chairman shouted, 'Order, Order!' and resumed in his quiet way. 'Our people, it is enough. The Intruder spoke well. Let's look into what he has said.' There was more noise, but soon, they were quiet again. Someone raised his hand. It was the same man, Ezeama whose two children were officers. He was looking so well that his sons must be looking after him.

'I think the Intruder spoke well,' the Chairman said. 'In wars, we make room for possible evacuation. The soldiers are here with us. They will fight. The women and children, and I should add the aged, should be evacuated should Ugwuta be threatened. But God forbid. Uhamiri forbid.'

'Chairman, no! no! no! You are misleading us. This man is misleading us, my people. Let's not hear him.' It was the woman politician, Madam Agafa again. 'What is all this? I don't like the way this meeting is going. We have come to discuss serious matters and people here are trying to sabotage every effort to arrive at any decision. I am a woman. I am not afraid of shelling. I am not afraid of any Vandal. I am going to fight with my mortar pistol. She turned in the direction of the women. 'Isn't that what you said I should say?'

'Yes, yes,' filled the air. 'That's exactly what we said you should say.' Another woman got up and said, 'We are behind you.'

'Have you heard? Cowards in this hall. Have you heard, Chairman?' She glowered daringly at the people and then began quietly, 'I am a woman. But I am not going to be evacuated. Have you heard? We women are solidly behind our men. Our children will be with us. Have you heard? My five children will be with me. We are not going to leave

12

Ugwuta for the vandals. God is on our side. Our cause is just. We shall vanquish.

'Who are these Nigerians, these Vandals, these Hausas? Didn't you read the story of David and Goliath? How David, because the Lord God was with him, slew Goliath with only a catapult . . .'

By now Chudi was as thoroughly fed up as I was. We wanted to leave, but dared not. A man had tried to leave, but was stopped.

'You mean to tell us that you want the Vandals to take our Ugwuta?'

The man stared back at the man who barred his way. 'No, of course not,' he said. He had his wits.

'Well, then, sit down, and listen. We have not come here to play.'

I began to blame myself for coming. I should not have accompanied Chudi. But I had nothing else to do. I was realising for the first time how idle one could be in time of war. It was the idleness more than anything else that bored people and led them to committing acts of lawlessness.

At home, those who did not carry arms had nothing to do. Only the women did some work. Well, some of them cooked for the soldiers, others traded with the enemy on the borders. They called it 'attack trade'. + ~these women would be discussing acts of acquisition English~

The meeting went on. But at long last, it was decided that nobody should be evacuated. The women and the children were to remain behind and help to sustain the soldiers. There were few soldiers in Ugwuta. The naval boys were there as well. It was not known whether they had arms to fight. Unfortunately it was Chudi who raised this question. Ezeama got up from his seat at once, 'You saboteur. Before the Vandals entered Port Harcourt, you fled. Yes, my people, two weeks before they entered Port Harcourt, this spineless man fled with his wife and children and all his property. He hid at home for a week. If you saw him by

13

chance, he told you he had just arrived and he was going back to Port Harcourt in an hour's time. You are a woman. Are you going to die twice? Why talk of arms? The Biafran government knows the importance of Ugwuta. The Government will send arms and soldiers to defend Ugwuta. It is not for idle men like you to talk about.'

He was well answered. There was nothing again to add by any one. My husband was boiling but said nothing. Then he got up and walked quietly to the door. The man barred the door. 'I'll fight you if you don't get out of my way.' The man surprisingly enough removed his ugly hand and he went out. It was too much for him. I let him go. One was enough. Two would be a crowd. Someone said, 'That's him going. *Sabo.* That's him going, And you, why did you allow him to go?' 'Leave him to go,' Madam Agafa said. 'Can he save Ugwuta? If he were my son, I would disown him in the market place.'

'Please let's go on with the meeting,' another from the crowd said.

The Chairman continued. They did not go very far when there was a big commotion again. Over what, nobody was able to say. I wondered why our people were so interested in meetings. Everybody would leave whatever he was doing to attend a meeting. What was the purpose of these meetings? During the war, there were so many that I wondered whether they were necessary. I didn't think that much could be achieved in mass meetings of this kind. Committees could achieve something. Later I had discussed this point with one of the leaders. It was after our discussion which went very well that the 'elites' decided to form a 'war cabinet'. My husband was not one of them. He was not an 'elite'. But it was our idea, and nobody remembered us. Obviously, we could not be trusted.

The meeting went on after the commotion, and plans were being made about what action to adopt should the Vandals invade us. Madam Agafa was speaking. Suddenly there was

14

dead silence as a soldier walked in, armed to the teeth. [...]
walked up to the Chairman who could be seen trembli[...]
Everybody was quiet as he whispered into the ear of [...]
Chairman. The people wondered why he could not ha[...]
spoken to the Army at their camp. He had no busin[...]
coming armed to the hall where civilians were meeting. [...]
should be disarmed first before he was allowed to come [...]
But who allowed him to come in, in the first place?

As he whispered to the Chairman, the frightened peop[...]
began to leave the hall one by one. Agafa was the first [...]
leave. Nobody knew really when she left. She was speaki[...]
when the soldier entered the hall. She must have a good
presence of mind. When others were held spell-bound she
disappeared.

The Chairman became more relaxed as the whispering
continued. There was no immediate danger, obviously. Then
the people saw the soldier move to another end of the hall
quite agitated and sad. A few people were consulted and
afterwards, the soldier was allowed to speak.

'I am from the war front', he began, in a dialect that was
difficult for the people to understand. They wondered which
war front he meant. There were so many war fronts. At the
beginning of the war when a soldier told you he was from a
war front, you gave him drinks if you met him in a pub. Or
you invited him to your home, and he ate with you and your
family. If he was an officer, and you had daughters, you did
not mind if he slept with one of them or even took her away
the next morning.

'I grew up in this town. My mother and father lived in
Umuosuma village. I am from Oburuoto.' The people were
very attentive. Oburuoto is just at the other side of the lake.
The people were their kith and kin. So the soldier was after
all their brother. 'I was fighting at Aba Sector when I was
called upon to fight in this Sector.' This again was not clear
to the people. Which sector was the man referring to? Surely

15

there was no fighting at Oburuoto.

Somebody got up. He must be a soldier who had returned home on leave. 'Before you go on, please disarm yourself. You are addressing civilians. You are not in a war front or addressing soldiers.' He sat down. The soldier apologised and removed his gun from his shoulder and placed it at one end of the hall far from the people.

'The Vandals are pushing on, and it is very likely that Oburuoto will be evacuated at any time. My men have no arms and ammunition to fight the Vandals. If this were another sector, I would have withdrawn my men. But this is my home and I want to save my fatherland. You have very influential people here. What I want you to do is to send some of your men to Umuahia and tell them that we have no arms and ammunition. That if I wait for twenty four hours and I don't get arms and ammunition, I am going to withdraw my men. They cannot fight without arms. These idle Nigerian officers don't want to fight. They send us to the war fronts to die. We are, after all, wartime officers and therefore inferior to them. They don't give us arms. They sit down at headquarters grumbling and drinking and what's more, when they see us with beautiful girls, they lock us up and take over our girls.'

'This is what we have been saying,' someone in the crowd said. 'There is no end to this sort of thing. That's why this war will never end. How can it end when officers behave in this way?' and others nodded in agreement.

'And again,' the soldier from Oburuoto continued, 'For the past twenty four hours, my soldiers have eaten nothing. They are very hungry, we have no food. The women who were cooking for us fled as the shelling became frequent. So I am asking you to please organise something for my boys to eat.

'I want to tell you that God is very powerful. It is not for a soldier to say this. But I will say it, the Vandals would have

16

taken Kalabari Beach three days ago, but for their foolishness. Oh, if only we could have one twentieth of the arms and the ammunition they have. We would have driven Lagos into the sea last year. They saw a mile post which read forty seven miles. They thought that Ugwuta was forty seven miles from the spot. So they decided to wait for four days before they started again. They did not know that Ugwuta was only seven miles from the spot.'

'Ignorant Vandals. What do they know? It's the British.' It was one of the elites who spoke. 'The war would have ended long ago but for the British, who are supplying arms to Nigeria. If it had been between us and Nigeria, the war would have ended ages ago. The British, they are causing all these troubles. You wait until we win. We will deal with the British.'

The Chairman and his supporters spoke in low tones, and when the hall was quiet, the Chairman spoke. They had heard what the soldier from the war front said. He wanted them to decide what they were to do. He wanted to let them realise that the man came to them voluntarily because he was one of them. And that they should treat him well, even though they might not believe what he had said to them.

Somebody from the audience got up, enumerated all that the soldier had said and sat down. What a waste of time. Another got up, spoke at length about the cause of the war, how he had fled from Jos and left behind him his property and his lucrative business, and sat down. There was no end to this. Then the Chairman said again.

'We have heard all this before. The soldier has made requests, are we going to do anything about these requests?' Someone got up again, and said, 'This is a military regime. We are at war with Nigeria. We must be very careful what we hear. I want to ask the soldier a few questions. The questions are: Who sent you here to address us? How did you know that we were having a meeting today and in this hall? My people, there is no substance in what this man has said to us. How could the Vandals come within seven miles of Ugwuta and no shelling was heard? Do the Vandals fly? Are they birds? The latest report we heard from Umuahia was that the Vandals were in Omoku. The gallant Biafran soldiers beat them back last night, and now they must be far, far away from Omoku. The sooner we stop listening to these deserters, the better for us. I came to this meeting hoping that something concrete would be decided. The only thing that is concrete is the decision that women and children should not be evacuated. I have been musing on the frailty of human beings. We have forgotten already why we are fighting. I know that there are some people here who will gladly go back to Nigeria if they have the means. I know of young men here who should be fighting, young women who should be organising the women, but choose to remain at home idling away precious time, and listening to gossip.

'Young soldier, go back to whence you came. We don't know you. You may be a saboteur, you may be a Nigerian who has infiltrated into our midst. You should be locked up. People like you should not be allowed to go about causing panic. Our people, I returned from Umuahia only yesterday. If I tell you what I saw with my own eyes, you will not believe it. Leave it at that. It is not for me to disclose. Ojukwu will make a broadcast. You wait until you hear the broadcast.

'I am glad that there are a group of men and women who are dedicated to the cause of Biafra. These men have sacrificed everything for Biafra. When I come here what I hear is evacuation, hunger, arms and ammunition. Young men of Ugwuta, I am ashamed of you. Imagine a woman intellectual the other day telling me that she was not doing any work. Such women should be locked up. Yes, whether married or not, whether a mother or not, they should be locked up as an example to others. We shall fight this war to the bitter end. No power in Black Africa will subdue us. I have been sent by the State House to organise the men of service to Biafra.'

The soldier from Oburuoto shook his head, picked up his gun and walked out of the hall. He headed for the ferry which took him to the other side of the river where his men were. The following day, hungry and tattered looking Biafran soldiers were seen along the road marching towards Mgbidi. The soldier from Oburuoto had withdrawn his men as he said. He could not fight without food, without arms and without ammunition.

When the soldier from Oburuoto left, the intellectual went up to the Chairman and spoke sternly to him. Few people heard what he said. When he finished, there were arguments here and there. A few hooligans shouted. The Chairman could no longer keep order. The meeting broke up. Everybody went home.

The following morning, very early, the bell man was heard saying: 'All young men and women are wanted in the School Hall this morning at ten. Those who are exempted from coming are the Ezechioha and the Nzeukwu age-grades.' (The two age-grades were over sixty five years old)

'This is very serious', I said to my husband. 'You have to go, don't you?'

'I will not go. They can come here and carry me, I am not stepping an inch from here. I don't want to be insulted by anybody again.'

'We are at war you know. There is no order. You have to go. When you go there, don't say anything to anybody to avoid being insulted.'

Chudi said nothing again, and I knew that I had won him over. At the appointed time, he was in the hall. Kal was there. Kal was as cunning as ever. He told my husband that he was going to remain behind and fight. It would be a shame if Ugwuta was taken by the Vandals.

The men who addressed the meeting were men from Umuahia. There were one or two officers with them who were in very well ironed and smart uniforms. They looked so well fed, and did not talk to anybody, not even the civilian intellectuals who had come with them.

It was a short meeting, comparatively speaking. The people were very brief and to the point. They were from Umuahia. They had gone to the other side of the river and seen the soldiers there. They had everything, food, drinks, arms and ammunition. They lacked nothing. The soldier who had tried to cause panic the day before had been dealt with in the usual way. And now they would get down to business. It was left to the young men and women of this historic town to show their patriotism and fight to the end. Victory would be theirs in the end. There was no doubt in their minds about the ultimate victory.

As for the Navy, Airforce and the Army in Ugwuta, arms and ammunition had been sent to them. Only two nights before, ten plane loads of arms and ammunition had landed safely in Uli airstrip. Why should the people of Ugwuta listen to gossips when they were next door to Uli, and heard planes landing and taking off all night long? After the address, they left and the people continued the business of the day.

'This is good talk, this is good talk,' the people said. How soothing it was. This was the kind of thing they wanted to hear, not lies told by deserters.

The meeting proved to be a great success for the intellectuals from Umuahia and Kal. Kal was at home with us. He did not travel much. But he did seem to have all the inside stuff. He did not talk much, though, and he had very few friends. Chudi was one of the few friends Kal had. But because of his deep involvement in the war, we began to be afraid of him and to see less of him. But he came occasionally

20

to us and we tried as much as possible not to discuss the war. There was no point at all discussing the war with Kal. He had answers to everything, to every question. When you eventually cornered him, he became angry and threatened to hand you over to the Army or to detain you. He appeared so powerful. Nobody seemed to know where he derived his power from. He did not seem to be very worried about our losses. There was always an answer.

After the meeting, he came up to us with a few friends. They were the people we knew fairly well. We talked about the good old days, trying to avoid the war. Then someone came in looking very cheerful. He was a civilian who worked closely with the Army.

'I am just from the war front,' he announced.

'Which one?' someone asked.

'There are so many now,' another put in.

I watched Kal. He was tense.

'Tell us quickly, where have we wiped them out?' I said flippantly, and Chudi nearly ordered me out of the room. The man did not seem perturbed. He went on: 'Umuokane, you know the place. Gallant Biafran soldiers wiped them all out. I am just from there. I don't think I can eat in the next three days.'

'There is very little to eat anyway,' I said to myself, feeling sick of all these lies and deceits.

'Where did you say we wiped them out?' someone asked.

'Umuokane,' the man repeated.

The Transport Directorate was there barely three weeks ago. Bee had told me about the place. She was there. Their Directorate moved there after Port Harcourt. There, she found peace for some time. It was a small village with a church and a school. She had found accommodation with a family of four. The woman was so good to her that she gave her one of the rooms to herself, while she, her husband and the children shared the other room. Every morning, the man

21

gave her a pot of fresh palm wine straight from the tree. Bee meant to remain there until the war ended. She thought the Federal troops would not get there. It was so remote. But she forgot that the Port Harcourt-Owerri Road was only five miles away.

So as soon as Umuokane was mentioned, I paid attention at once. 'Dead Vandals, all over the place, Nigeria is depopulated. Without exaggeration, I can say that there were over seven thousand dead Vandals there. The villagers were summoned to bury the dead. They were paid five shillings for every body buried. The Vandals will not attack for the next three months. Their losses were too much in that single encounter. They should not have struck when they did.'

I thought, seven thousand soldiers! Villagers burying the dead. It made no sense to me. Where were the villagers? Where was the battle field? How big was it to accommodate seven thousand corpses? There were some who thought that a battle field was like a football field. I watched my husband. He did not believe the man. I watched Kal. His face was blank.

That was Kal all over. The war had changed him a good deal. You can never know what he was thinking about. You could never read his face. He talked less, and was utterly unpredictable.

'Where are you going then?' Kal asked.

'Oh, to the Uli airstrip. Someone is giving a lot of trouble there. I am going to investigate.'

'Go quickly then before he bolts.'

'Oh, do you know the man?' he asked Kal.

'I don't know him. You can leave now, you are talking too much.'

That did not sound like Kal. What was he up to? Talking in that way? Well, one must be careful. We went on talking after the man had left. Nobody seemed to refer to the news just given during our discussions. It all implied that we were safe for the meantime. If the Vandals had succeeded, then it would mean that Owerri would be threatened. If Owerri was threatened, then Ugwuta was threatened.

We fell to talking about the BBC and its news. I said I took it very seriously. The view of the others was that I was a fool to take it seriously. The BBC was simply lying. Nigeria was not preparing any attack on Ugwuta. It was just not possible. 'But we heard the Nigerians were making arrangements for flat bottomed boats for the attack,' I insisted.

'Lies, all lies,' many said. I did not want to talk much. I kept quiet.

Kal and the Intellectual had organised the young men. In the morning, one saw them parading on the school ground. Meanwhile the 'War Cabinet' had been formed. Kal and the Intellectual were members. Membership was restricted. The heads of the Airforce, the Navy and the Army were members. The Divisional Officer was a member as well, and so were other very prominent people of Ugwuta. Every night they met to discuss the war situation. They visited the war fronts, giving encouragement to the boys who were fighting and arranging for arms and ammunition to be sent from Umuahia.

I was very happy about this. At least something concrete, sensible and tangible was being done. At long last the people who mattered were now thinking. We were no longer fighting with mere words. Words were impotent. Biafra could not win a civil war by mere words. How I longed to say that to Ojukwu. But who was I? And besides, it was too late, too damn late. We had already lost the war. We lost the war when we lost Port Harcourt. It was sheer madness fighting after Port Harcourt. All right-thinking people knew this. What we should have done was surrender. Surrender;

23

nobody in Biafra could say that word openly and remain alive. He would be torn to pieces in the market place. Surrender! Surrender and be slaughtered by the Vandals. If we surrendered, we would all be butchered. It was strong and thoughtful propaganda. And . . . it worked!

The people in the 'War Cabinet' were very responsible people. They had a programme. There was order. They came together each night and reviewed the war situation. The three heads supplying the details and asking for help from the natives where they needed help.

It was the training that I thought was rather funny.

'Where are these people going to find the arms and ammunition?' I asked the Intellectual one morning when. accompanied by Kal, he came to complain that Chudi did not turn out for the training.

'Arms and ammunition?' he replied curtly. 'You do the training first, Umuahia will supply the arms and the ammunition. Don't bother yourself with that. OK? Nobody will run. We all will be here. We are going round telling people that anybody seen running will be shot. We are going to defend our fatherland, all right? Look at Vietnam. They have been at war for the past thirty-five years. Thirty-five years, and they are still fighting. How long have we fought? Only one year. Just one single year and we are already tired. There are young men and women like us in Vietnam who have known no peace since they were born. They are fighting. Still fighting to free their fatherland from American imperialism.'

'I know you are well read in these things,' Chudi replied. 'I am not an intellectual like you, but I read a bit of history. You should not compare Biafra with Vietnam. We seceded from Nigeria only one and a half years ago. We have built nothing. And remember we are blockaded. I keep on saying that but for the blockade, we would not have lost the war. And besides –' He couldn't finish.

'Are you saying that we have lost the war?' Kal interrupted.

'I am not saying that.' My husband was uncomfortable. He should not have said that.

'Kal, that was not what Chudi said,' I ventured to say. Kal's face was again blank. He ignored me completely.

'Let's go,' he said to the Intellectual. 'I don't know what Kate and her husband are turning into.'

'I think it is high time they were handed over to the Army or to the D.M.I. They should be locked up somewhere. They are becoming very dangerous,' the Intellectual from Umuahia said.

'Not yet. Let's not recommend that yet. They don't know that Ojukwu has the file of everybody in Biafra. One day they will betray themselves and the D.M.I. will arrest them. They are damn saboteurs. I won't be surprised if I wake up one morning and hear that they had gone back to Nigeria, these people.'

So saying, they stumped out.

One night, there was shelling. I was unable to sleep. I woke Chudi several times. He heard the shelling, hissed and went back to sleep. I envied him as he slept. I went over to the next room where our children were sleeping. Good children, they were all fast asleep. They were lucky children who didn't seem to know the danger we were in. Our flights had been so exciting to them. They had not started to suffer as grown ups were suffering. If the war lasted another year, they would begin to suffer, first from hunger, discomfort and then ill health. I was determined not to see my children suffer. I would sell all I had to feed them if I had to. They were not going to be hungry. They would not suffer from kwashiorkor. Heavens, no. Kwashiorkor was a deadly disease of children, more deadly in Biafra then leprosy. Leprosy was not feared any more. Lepers mingled with people these days. A leper was once conscripted into the army. He protested that he was a leper; he was told that he was lying. And even if he were leper, he would die one day any way. And it was better, more noble to die fighting for Biafra than as a miserable leper.

In the morning, the shelling continued intermittently. I was very nervous. I could hardly sit or stand. I tried to pack. Packing was impossible. What and what was I going to take? I went to see my mother after breakfast. She looked tired and worried. Her waist was still bulging. Papa went to a meeting.

'Meetings, these people do nothing but attend meetings,' I complained. 'Did you hear the shelling last night?' I asked my mother.

'I heard it. But they said "our people" were shelling.'

'Are they shelling who?' I asked holding my anger.

'Nigerians of course,' my mother said, equally angry.

'The Nigerians are shelling us. The Vandals are shelling us. Don't be deceived. If Biafran soldiers were shelling, then it meant that the Vandals were near. Can't you see?'

'How do you know that they are near?' my mother asked.

For a second I was afraid. Am I not talking with my own mother? My God, is the propaganda affecting my mother? How do I know that they are near? How can I answer that question? That's the question people asked you when you told them that a place had fallen or was about to fall. Only saboteurs knew when a place was about to fall.

'Mama, I don't like this question,' I said to my mother. I was hurt.

'Kate,' she said. 'I don't like the way you are behaving of late. You frightened us by saying that the Nigerians were attacking us by water. Are they here now?'

'The war is not yet over, they will come.'

'You must be very careful what you say these days,' she warned. 'You are not the most sensible person in Ugwuta today. Those people who died in Enugu, those who were shot, were shot because they said the Nigerians would take

26

Enugu and we had lost the war'.

'Nigerians did take Enugu, and we are losing the war,' I said. If my own mother handed me over to the Army, then the world had come to an end. I'll make a painful exit. But I must talk to my mother. Then a thought struck me. Why should I talk? There was no point. Why should I argue with her? When the time came to run, she would run. Nobody will tell her not to run.

'Never mind me, Mama,' I said. 'I have come to tell you to be ready in case we have to run. I am trying to put one or two .nings together. Tell your sister and brother to get ready in case we have to run. But God forbid that we should run.'

'That's what I am saying, my child. God forbid that we should run, We are not going to run. The other day, the women offered a white ram to the Woman of the Lake. I was there. Every village was asked to do this. Those who could not afford a white ram, were asked to offer a white cock. She will not let us down. The Woman of the Lake loves her children. She will protect her children from the hands of the Vandals. There is God. The Nigerians have treated us like dirt. God will revenge. God will vindicate our cause. My daughter, tell me, you who went to school. Why won't they leave us alone? We have left them in Nigeria. They said we grabbed everything; we have said: all right, you are killing us because we grabbed everything. We are not going to grab any more. We are going home. They say: now come back otherwise we will bring you back by force. And they are still killing us. They don't want us, yet they won't let us alone to fend for ourselves. That's why, my daughter, I am at a loss what to do in this war. Do they want us back, so that they can kill all of us, wipe out the whole race?'

'Don't worry,' I consoled my mother. She was right. What did she know about the war? What did she know about the causes of the war and the events that led to it? You didn't get up one morning and start shooting people because you were a soldier and had access to arms.

'Don't worry,' I said again. 'You and I do not understand. All that is left now, is to keep alive. This is not the time to apportion blame. Let's keep alive first. Perhaps at the end of this calamity, this tragedy, if we are alive, we shall be able to find answers to these questions.'

As we were talking, one of my mother's friends came in. She was from the farm, and so her dress was tattered and dirty. 'Are you just returning from the farm?' my mother asked her. She did not like seeing her in tattered clothes. 'Yes,' she said.

'Why then don't you have on something respectable to wear? What is the matter?' my mother asked.

The woman hissed, then said simply, 'My son is missing.' The woman had only one son, who should be about twenty eight years old.

'How missing?' I asked frightened.

'We were returning from the farm when we heard a shot. My son was behind. We began to run. The young men overtook me. I managed to continue running until I got to the river. There were several others before me. It was when we got to the river that we knew what it was. The Nigerians, they said, are in a school room in Osu Obodo.'

'Osu Obodo? Impossible!' I exclaimed. 'Osu Obodo! No, That's too near,' I said again.

My mother motioned the woman to go on. 'It was at the river side that a young man from our farm told me that my son was locked up in the school room because he wouldn't tell the soldiers the direction of Ugwuta.'

'The direction? But they were in Ugwuta. If they were in Osu Obodo, then they had arrived Ugwuta.'

'Well, so they told me. Up till now, I have not seen my son. My son has been killed by the Hausas. My daughter who lived in Vom did not return, and now my son. What interest had I in the politics of the country, and now this has befallen me, an insignificant wretch like me. What am I to do?'

My mother consoled her, telling her that her son would return. That it was not true that the Nigerians had taken him prisoner. It would be all right. She should not worry.

I had different versions of this story by the time I got home that morning. The radio was on and there was a war report. I heard 'Oguta Sector' and my blood ran cold. Hitherto 'Biafran Radio' had not admitted that any fighting was going on in Ugwuta. It had always said that fighting was going on in Omoku. That meant that there was some truth in what the woman had said. 'The gallant Biafran soldiers had wiped out the Vandals in Oguta Sector. An eye-witness report said that the gallant Biafran soldiers freed ten men who were held as hostages in a school room in Obukofia. Thousands of arms and ammunition were seized from the Vandals. It was pertinent to remind listeners what the Biafran Head of State had said that we didn't buy our arms and ammunitions from overseas. We seize them from the Vandals.'

Chudi was very sad. He had gone up to the field to see what the youths were doing. They had wooden sticks as guns on their shoulders. A wounded Biafran soldier was in command. He limped as he commanded and it was so painfully ridiculous that my husband turned back and went home.

How could those people he saw defend Ugwuta? What were the people, the soldiers who were paid to defend us doing? They were not doing anything at all. And yet there was a strong campaign that anybody seen packing would be handed over to the Army. Every day, the bell man went round jingling his bell and assuring everybody that all was going very well. Nobody would be allowed to leave. The youths were determined to defend our fatherland.

There was shelling again in the morning. It continued all day. Very few people seemed to be bothered by it. The day was Nkwo, and the market place was filled with people. I was ill at ease. Then Bee came. I did not know she was coming. For once I did not welcome Bee properly. 'We weren't expecting you.' I blurted out. Then I told her I was sorry. I was under tension.

'I heard the Vandals had taken Ugwuta, so I came. People do tell a lot of lies these days.'

'They will take it any time now,' I said.

Then: *gbim, gbim*. The ground shook. Bee rushed to the toilet.

'You see, they are here, make no mistake about it, any day from now, they will land.'

'What arrangements are you making for evacuation then?' Bee asked me when she returned from the toilet.

'We are footing it,' I said sadly. 'We have no petrol, they wouldn't sell petrol. At the last meeting the people had, we begged them, I mean we who had fled many times, but they refused. They have been instructed not to sell petrol to anyone. Anyone who was seen trafficking in petrol would be handed to the Army. I have never seen anything like this before. The Nigerians have robbed us of everything including our commonsense. What annoys me most is that those on the Petrol Committee know what it is to run. Some of them were in Port Harcourt when the Vandals came. They should realise by now that when the Vandals say that they will take a place, they will take it even if it costs them all their men and it takes months to take the place.'

'I can help you with petrol,' Bee said. 'There is a place nearby where I can buy petrol. Just give me the money, black market price.'

I gave Bee the money and that evening she got us four gallons of petrol. 'Don't ask me where I bought it,' she said smiling. Then she came near and whispered the name of the person who sold it to her. My blood ran cold.

The following day, my husband took out the car to see

whether it would start at all. It started. He drove it to my mother's and came back.

'We are set' he said. 'We should get everything ready in case.'

'Nothing will happen,' Bee said.

'Yes, nothing will happen, but it won't be out of place if we got ready in case anything does happen,' Chudi said.

We heard Kal's voice. He was angry. 'You all are saboteurs. All of you. You are going to suffer. You, why didn't you go for combing? Didn't you hear that there are infiltrators in Ugwuta? Ten were caught only last night. Young men have been combing the town and the bushes since morning, and you are here doing nothing as if the imminent fall of Ugwuta did not matter to you.' Kal was talking to someone, but we knew circumstances.

'Even if they were being mortared?' my husband asked

'Yes, even if they were being mortared. Mortared you say? Ignorant Nigerians, spineless Vandals, uncircumcised idiots, kolanut eaters. Mortared you say? Have they mortar bombs? Who gave them mortar bombs? They can't make a pin. Didn't you hear Gowon the other day on Radio Nigeria scolding Nigerian Scientists for their indolence? They cannot manufacture a pin. Our gallant Biafran scientists have made bombs, hand grenades, guns and shore batteries. Name it and our boys have made it. What have the Nigerian scientists made? Nothing. All they've done since the war began was quarrel.' His words and anger were directed at Chudi and me. He had clashed openly with Chudi the day before. And he had threatened him with detention. Chudi had gone to him and appealed to him to please stop the propaganda of asking the people not to run. He had told him that it was a great disservice to the people, the cause and to his own conscience. There had been a bitter argument, but at the end of it they had parted as friends.

Chudi had said that the only sensible thing to do was to

prepare the people for possible evacuation. There was no point at all in telling them to defend their fatherland. That it was not a shame if they fled from their fatherland when it was obvious that if the Vandals did come, nobody, not even the soldiers nor Kal himself would remain to fight them. There were so many aged and children who should be evacuated, and the sooner they did it the better. Kal had maintained that the people should stay and defend their homeland under any circumstances, not run after women and give their extravagant parties. We will get even with them when this war is over.

'If you win, that is,' Chudi said. He regretted saying it soon after.

Kal did not speak for a minute or so. Then he said quietly, concealing his anger: 'We shall win. We are going to win. All these are setbacks. There is no doubt in my mind. We shall defeat the Nigerians in this war. No doubt at all. There must be setbacks in wars. Today we have our setbacks. But it is only temporary. So rest assured, we shall win.'

'But what if the Vandals start mortaring us from the other side of the Lake?' asked Chudi. It was a pointless question. But he was only trying gropingly to take back what he'd said.

'They have no mortar bombs. We have mortar bombs. My friend, I have just returned from Umuahia. I saw with my eyes the arms and ammunition that were there. But if they have mortar bombs, as you fear, the bombs will not land on Ugwuta soil. They will fly over.'

'And land where?'

'They will not land here I say, but somewhere else.'

'Not in Biafra?' Everybody was fighting for himself these days. If your home had not fallen, then you were not identified with the cause.

'We shall fight to the last man,' Kal said.

'Yes, the Vandals will kill us to the last man. Didn't you hear what Radio Televison Kaduna said?'

'Yes, you shall die to the last man. I heard them all right. So you still listen to Radio Television Kaduna. No wonder.'

'No wonder what?' my husband asked angrily. But Kal was not prepared for any physical showdown. Adroitly, he changed the topic and in the end they parted as friends . . .

'Combing,' I said. 'So there were infiltrators.' That convinced me that Ugwuta would fall. It was the same story. News of infiltration always heralded the fall of a place. There were infiltrators in Port Harcourt. They were caught and handed over to the Army. In some cases the people took the law into their own hands.

I asked Kal to come in. He would not come in. He wanted to go back to continue the combing, and wanted Chudi to go with him.

'My husband will not go with you,' I said. I was surprised at my boldness. 'Tell whoever sent you that my husband will not come with you to the combing. Why are you combing? Don't you hear? Don't you hear the shelling? There are no infiltrators here. Arrange evacuation of everybody including the men and the youths. Yes, the youths. Why should they die for nothing . . .'

'You mean that dying for Biafra is dying for nothing?'

'I don't mean that. What I mean is that it is wrong to allow men to die defenceless.'

'We are going to arm them.'

'With what?'

'Guns.'

'There are no guns. Please, Kal, why won't you save these people? You know there are no guns. You know that anybody who remains here when the Vandals come will die. You know! Why don't you do something?'

'You are getting mad, Kate, and your husband too is getting mad.'

'You are the one who is mad, not us, not my husband and I and Bee. We are normal, you are insane. And . . .'

33

Before I finished, Chudi had taken Kal away. He told him I'd had a very bad night. I had not slept at all because of the shelling. That was why I was talking in the way I did.

Bee did not leave. She preferred to remain with us to see the end. She wanted to report everything that happened. The car was ready, we had petrol and it could start. The bell man had warned car owners that if they attempted to run away they would have their tyres punctured. Everybody was to stay. Everything would be taken care of.

All day I was irritable. Perhaps I was getting mad. What was actually wrong with me? Was I really getting off my head? Everybody could not be mad at the same time. Perhaps it was I, I getting mad.

Bee remained for two days and nothing happened. So she decided to leave in the morning. That night, at about ten, we heard heavy knocks on the door.

'If you don't open the door, we shall break it.'

'Please don't break it,' we heard my mother-in-law saying. 'Please don't break it. I am coming to open it.' She opened the door. We all were out of bed now, including my children. Bee was also out of bed.

'We have come for combing,' one of the men said. It was the Intruder.

'For combing?' my husband asked.

'Yes, for combing. Don't you hear me? Have I water in my mouth. Are you not an Ugwuta man?'

I nudged Chudi and he understood. The men were allowed to search the house. That was why they came, to search for infiltrators hidden in our house. Who must have done this? Whose handiwork is this? We dared not say anything lest we would be in trouble. The men went from room to room. My husband followed them. Then suddenly, the Intruder asked, 'Why are you following us?'

'This is my house,' Chudi said quietly. 'You have your men with you. I am not interfering with your work.'

The Intruder and his men did not like this. But they went on searching. What were they searching for? What were they after? Did they think that we were going to hide anybody in a house like this? I could not understand it. Their intrusion remined me of Port Harcourt. A week before the Vandals shelled Port Harcourt, some Militia men had come to our house at two in the morning. They were searching for infiltrators. They searched for about ten minutes and went away. When they left, I asked Chudi what prevented these people from robbing or even killing us?

Nothing was private any more. We had lost our freedom and democracy. We lost them the day that the Army took over. January 15 1966, was the day when we lost our hard-earned freedom. There was nothing we could do about it. Everyone distrusted everyone else. Going from Owerri to Ugwuta, a distance of some twenty miles, one was searched at least six times. I wondered at the great enthusiasm the Civil Defenders, both men and young girls, had for ladies' handbags. Before one got to a Check Point, one saw hands outstretched for one's handbag. What was concealed in women's handbags?

Of course they found nothing. Our suitcases were not packed. So they could not accuse us of packing, ready to flee. Just when they were about to leave, one of them noticed Bee. 'Where are you from, you are not an Ugwuta woman?' one of the men asked.

'No, she is not from Ugwuta,' Chudi volunteered to say.

'She has a mouth,' the Intruder snapped. 'Let her speak.'

'I am from Umuahia,' Bee said, trembling.

'You are not from Umuahia. Say where you came from.'

'I said I was from Umuahia. I am a native of Umaunachi though. I work in Umuahia.'

'Why did you tell us you were from Umuahia then?'

'I am sorry, I am from Umunachi. I didn't understand your question at first.'

'We spoke in Ibo. Aren't you Ibo?'

'I am Ibo of course. I said I didn't understand your question at first. Is this the way you treat visitors here? This is rather strange.'

'You are saying this. You must come with us then to the camp,' the Intruder said.

'We have had enough of this,' Chudi said. 'I am not a stranger in this town. I was born and bred here, and Bee is our guest. If you don't stop molesting her, I am going to report you all to the Chairman.' They merely laughed. 'The Chairman did not send us,' meaning the Chairman of the Civil Defence Committee.

'Who sent you then at the dead of night?'

'We have not come here to answer questions. This woman must come with us. She is going to be interrogated. We do not know why she is here.'

'You think she is an infiltrator?' I asked.

'Yes,' one of the men said. 'Don't you see how well she is looking, when we are fighting. She must be an infiltrator to look so well'.

'Christ. What has gone wrong?' Chudi asked in exasperation. 'You are not taking her away from this house. You will kill all of us here before you take her away.'

'Let me go with them,' Bee said. 'Why all the fuss, I'll be back. I know I am not a Nigerian but a Biafran. I'll be back.' But I could see the pain in her voice. She was experiencing this raw deal for the first time since the war began.

The men were sent by Kal just to embarrass us and Bee whom he had fallen out with. Bee had told us that she had nothing to do with Kal any more. That Kal was a liar, an impostor and a fake. We did not believe all that she said though, but we were sure that the men were sent by Kal.

The men left after a long time of pleadings from my mother-in-law and the others living on the compound. The following morning Bee left.

We had asked one of the members of the 'War Cabinet' to give Bee a lift to Umuahia. He had agreed but said he was not leaving the town until after the meeting of the 'War Cabinet' as he wanted to know more about what was going on at the fronts. There was a meeting that night, and after it he came to see us. Bee had gone then. She probably would announce at Umuahia that nothing was happening in Ugwuta.

Mike was one of those who had some balance of some sort in the then Biafra. Of course he behaved like everybody else until Calabar fell. His wife, right from the word go, could not live down the propaganda. She so criticised everything that went on that Mike barred her from participating in conversations on the war. Mike's wife had obeyed like the good wife she was. She did not want their twelve years of married bliss to be terminated by the Biafran war.

So when the young men at Enugu were buying guns, she bought a gun for her husband, and even helped to build a bunker at the back of their house. When the bunker was ready she could not help asking her husband if the bunker and the gun would be needed. Mike had sensed what she was driving at. There was a lot of cynicism in her question. He answered truthfully. 'When you are firing at the enemy in a bunker with your family in it, then the end is near.'

His wife had hissed and went on with her sewing. Mike left his house intact, the gun included, when Enugu fell. He never had an opportunity to use either the gun or the bunker.

Mike was at the meeting, and when it was over, he came to tell us. Bless him, he came to tell us. Things were very bad. He was not happy with the reports. All three were contradictory. Because of these contradictions, Mike had decided to remain behind in case he had to evacuate his family. He did not see how this was possible, but in war anything was possible.

The amphibious attack of Ugwuta was coming though. The Airforce Officer had reported that he saw nothing that was alarming in Egbema. There were no flat-bottomed boats in sight at all. The naval officer reported that there was an attack by the Vandals by water in Egbema. In actual fact, there were four boats. Two were knocked out outright. The shore-batteries performed as usual. The other two had escaped. The Army Officer said that his men were holding solidly on the Egbema front, and there was no cause for alarm at all.

None of these accounts was satisfactory to Mike. So he had decided to remain behind. If it was true that two escaped destruction, where did they flee too? Obviously they did not make their way back to Port Harcourt creeks. They were near and bound to try again. That was how Mike saw the danger. God bless Mike. The message went home immediately. My husband and I were excited. We wanted to start moving that night but there was no point. The people would murder us if they saw us running away when on the surface everything was going according to plan.

We went to our mother and told her. 'This is what we heard, anything can happen. So if you gave anybody money for Umuonya better go and get it back from her. The Nigerians it is feared, may come.' My mother-in-law rushed to her daughter and told her: 'Didn't we say that Chudi and his wife will kill you. Is that why you are coming to us in the dead of the night. Dead Nigerians, can't come. The BBC said they would come, they are not here yet. Our forces are ready for them. The shore-batteries are there. Please go and sleep.'

My mother-in-law rushed back. But then I had gone to tell my mother. When I finished telling her, she knelt down and prayed. After praying, she said, 'Nothing will happen, Kate. God forbid that anything should happen. We can't leave Ugwuta. No, we can't leave Ugwuta for the Nigerians. Every place can fall, not Ugwuta. Only the night before, we sacrificed again to the Woman of the Lake. The . . .'

'You went with them. Christ! Mama, did you go with

them? You are no longer a Christian? You could go with the heathens to the shrine of the Woman of the Lake to sacrifice to her.'

'I can do anything to save Biafra, do you hear, and stop coming here and causing panic, Kate.' That was my mother.

Chudi was arguing with my mother-in-law in a low tone of voice. 'We didn't tell you that the Vandals were coming in actual fact. We told you to get ready if they did come. You gave your money to somebody who is going to Umuonya tomorrow. It is a large sum of money, you told me. It is safer if you go and get if from her. It could get lost if the Vandals did come. Who wants the Vandals to come, any way. Who wants to leave his home to be a refugee elsewhere? Not me. Yet if we are forced to abandon our homes to save our lives, we have no alternative.'

My mother-in-law was utterly confused. She rushed back to her daughter Sue, who scolded her and then came to us to scold us. My husband was not in the mood to argue. When his sister finished talking to him, he said quietly, 'I am not asking you to leave Ugwuta with me. You can stay if you like. Your husband is not here. If anything happens and you are unprepared, you are going to lose a lot. Get prepared first, that is all we are saying.

'But the Nigerians cannot come. It is not possible. Didn't you hear how we slaughtered them at Omoku and Ibeocha. In fact it is hoped that our troops will recapture Port Harcourt in a week.'

'Oh, so you now believe that Port Harcourt is in the hands of the Vandals. I thought you said we were cowards when we abandoned Port Harcourt, that the Vandals were not in Port Harcourt and that only the saboteurs were causing trouble. Let me tell you, we will not see Port Harcourt until the war ends. That is if we survive till then.'

'Chudi, you must continue your packing,' I called from the next room.

Sue came into the room where I was packing. I thought she was angry with me until she said, 'Did you say we can't contain them?'

'It is not likely,' I said. 'They are already in Oburuoto. If they are not attacked tonight, then they will be here by tomorrow. And who is going to resist them?'

'Aren't our soldiers fighting any more?' my sister-in-law asked. Obviously she was getting afraid now.

'They are fighting. This not the time to ask questions. Please go home and start packing. If we are lucky and the Biafran forces wipe them out, all well and good. After all, who wants to be a refugee?'

'But where are you going?' Sue asked. She was thinking of her five little children. Her husband Pat was employed with the Fuel Directorate, far away at Umuahia.

'We don't know yet. The important thing is to get out of here first. Perhaps we are all going to stay in a village school room,' I said. I remembered the refugees I saw at the beginning of the war. I never thought then that I too would be a miserable refugee in Biafra.

'I am not going to run. Where will I run to? I cannot leave Ugwuta,' Sue said.

'That's your own business,' Chudi said. 'Your business and nobody else's. And good luck,' he added sternly and went on packing.

I could see that Chudi was angry. But what could he do? If his sister did not want to leave, he was not going to make her leave. Meanwhile, she went to my mother-in-law. She too was packing. 'So, you are going to leave? she asked.

'What can we do, if they come, we have to leave? But my mind tells me that we are not going to run. I believe strongly in the Woman of the Lake. She is not going to let us down. *Ewoo*, who brought this war on us? Is this the world? How can I leave the land of my birth for the Nigerians? No, it is not possible. It is just not possible.' She soliloquised for a long time, her daughter watching her. Then when she came to her senses, she shouted at her: 'Are you still here? Go home and pack. Your husband is not at home. Go and pack. Get your children out of danger. That is the important thing. That is if they come. But they will not come. The Nigerians will not come.'

When Sue got home, Pat was home too. But he was as mad as a bull.

'Who told you that?' Pat asked heaving out of bed.

'Everybody in town says it. Many are packing,' Sue said.

'Who are packing? I know your brother and his wife have already left the town,' he said.

'They have not left but they too are packing.'

'They are saboteurs, all those who are packing are saboteurs. The D.M.I. will deal with them. I am from Umuahia. There is nothing at all to alarm anybody. The enemy is at Omoku. They are being attacked this night, a brigade attack. They will be wiped out from Omoku tonight. I know all this because I work with the Fuel Directorate. We supplied fuel to those transporting our soldiers to Omoku. Tomorrow morning, I am going to Uli.'

'But you have to leave the car and the driver in case anything did happen,' Sue said.

'I am going for an important assignment. And besides I have told you that there is nothing at all. There is no danger.'

'We have been hearing shelling all this week. It will be easier to get out if you leave the car for us.'

'Ugwuta is not in danger. I have told you. You women worry too much. I am leaving very early tomorrow morning.'

Sue was very sad about this but there was nothing she could do. She could not persuade her husband to leave the car, or convince him that there was danger.

We had wanted to pack the cases into the car that night, but thought better of it.

I had persuaded Chudi not to because our neighbours

41

could hear us and wonder what we were up to. Also, from observations, we had noticed that the Nigerians did not fight at night. At night they went to sleep. It was the Biafrans who fought at night. If they were coming, they would come in broad daylight.

There was no sleep that night. The following morning we woke up hoping that all would be well. I had packed all the children's clothes in one suitcase. And another suitcase was used in packing my husband's clothes and mine. All the other belongings were food and cooking utensils. The car was small and we hadn't thought of my mother-in-law's things.

Luckily I asked her that morning to let me see what she was taking with her. She pointed to her trunk box, and chop box. I told her she could not take them as there was no room in the car unless she wanted to walk. She was so worried that she began to cry. I consoled her. I told her that we might not run after all. She said she was confident that we were not going to run. That the Woman of the Lake was not going to let us down. Her clothes were tied up in a bed sheet.

'Where are we running to?' She asked. I told her we did not know. All we knew was that if it were necessary to run, we would run. Fleeing from one's own home was not fun. 'We can't even run to the farm?' She wondered.

'No, we can't run to the farm,' I said, thinking of the elaborate preparations we had made as soon as Port Harcourt fell. A relation of my husband who was a farmer was given some money to build us a hut on the farm in case we had to flee from Ugwuta. He had promised to put up something quite modest. He kept demanding so much money from us that my husband decided to see the hut himself. When he got there, no hut was erected. The man was nowhere to be found. And we did not get our money back.

42

'What are we going to eat then if we leave Ugwuta?' my mother-in-law asked.

'God will provide,' I said, for want of any other thing to say.

I went to my mother and saw that she was quite ready. She was still worried. One of her sisters came. She was a sister as well as a friend to my mother. She was rich and influential. She had on a beautiful wrappa which she inherited from their mother. Coral beads and rich gold trinkets dangled from her neck. She returned my greeting cheerfully. She was not by nature a cheerful woman.

'We are not going to run,' she said to me.

'Auntie, who wants to run?' I said to her.

'I am not going to run. There are many like me who are not going to run. We dare the Nigerians to come. I am old, but I am going to kill one with my pistol before they kill me. Come, my daughter, where are we running to? The son of Izebunka has asked us not to run. That man has always said reasonable things since the war began. He and his friends went from house to house at dead of night asking us not to leave our fatherland. Strengthening us. It is what we need at this time. Not alarming stories, not evacuation. Evacuation. After all that the Hausas had done to us. After killing all our people in the North, and swearing that they would kill everybody above the age of five in Biafra. No, my daughter I am staying here. Many of us will be here.'

So that was what Kal and his friends did the previous night – Kal who left Port Harcourt even before us. Kal who had heard the shelling, who was in a position to understand. Was Kal going to remain in Ugwuta to see the Vandals enter? There was nothing that the son of Izebunka would not do. What was he after? Who would remember him when the war was won? And how could the war be won when we had lost Calabar and Port Harcourt? I just could not understand.

When my aunt left, I told my mother that I was afraid.

43

There was something about my aunt that was strange. She must be persuaded to leave if anything did happen. I decided to follow her to her house. When I got there, her husband was in. He too was well dressed though not cheerful. When I told him about my fears, he said quietly to me. 'I am an old man. I must die. If I have to die, then why not now? I am not going to leave my fatherland. God forbid, our ancestors forbid that I should leave the land of my birth. I am going to die here. Right here. Let them come. Come, my child. Have you seen those refugees in the school hall? When we leave here, we are going to be like them. We are going to be worse even, because we will not see water to drink let alone wash our clothes. I'll rather die here, than live the miserable life of a refugee. If I open my eyes and don't see water I'll die.'

He was a very clean man. His clothes were never dirty. He lived a clean and modest life. And I knew that rather than leave Ugwuta he would die in Ugwuta.

'We can go where there is water,' I said.

'Where?' he asked as if he did not hear me. Then he went on. 'You know I have never left Ugwuta. I don't know Ukwokwe. Those people who live beyond Ukwokwe have no water. It is like asking a fish to live out of water. I'll die in the first week. My ancestors forbid. I am not going to die in a strange land where there is no water. There will not be water to wash my dead body.'

I saw the pain in his eyes. He did not want to say it, but I knew that he remembered his son who was in Kano. He had not returned. He might have been killed by the Hausas. 'But,' I began, 'we can go to a place where there is water.'

'Where?' he asked. But he was not interested.

'Osomala for instance,' I said.

'Osomala,' he said. 'That's a possible place. But how do we get there? The Nigerians you say are coming by water. We can get to Osmala only when we go by the Lake.'

'No, we can go by land,' I told him.

'How?' he asked, with an interest that bordered on excitement.

'We can travel to Atani, then by the River Niger to Osomala.' He called his wife.

'Do you hear what your sister's daughter is saying?'

'I heard her all right. You can go with her if you like. I am going to die here.'

'Don't talk like that, my wife. Nobody really wants to die. Come, my child, are you sure the Nigerians will be here?' He was confused.

'I am not sure. Nobody is sure of anything. All that I know is that if the Nigerians come, we shall flee to a place of safety.'

Then someone came in. He did not like seeing me there, but he ignored me. 'We are going round,' he said. Then more people came in. They were all in shorts, and had their knives. 'We are going round,' he said again, 'to strengthen our people. Nobody should run if shooting was heard. The soldiers are all set for battle. We the youths are determined to give the last drop of our blood for Ugwuta. And we are going to succeed.'

My heart lost several beats. I had a secret hope that we might not run after all. I had put my hope on the brigade attack of last night, though I did not tell anybody. Secretly, I was hoping that the gallant Biafran soldiers would beat back the Vandals. The propaganda of these people had told me that all was not well. We couldn't win a civil war with mere impotent words, meaningless words. We would win with guns, guns – and arms and ammunition. God was on the side of the battalion who had superior weapons. We couldn't fight with pistols and matchets.

When they left, spreading their empty consoling words as they went, my aunt turned to her husband: 'Did you hear them? We have said that we would remain behind. I am set to die. But of course they will not come.'

45

Tears filled my eyes. The brigade attack had failed, that is, if there was a brigade attack at all. From then on, I was absolutely sure that we were going to flee from Ugwuta. My hopes had been dashed to pieces.

The market place was full of people. They were buying and selling. Tears filled my eyes as I picked my way among the crowd of market women. In a short time, there would be a stampede. Many people there would not be able to go back to their homes to take anything. Many would leave their wares behind and run empty handed. Many would die in the stampede.

I heard my name. The person must have been calling for a long time. It was Mike's wife. She was a bit agitated as she carried a huge basket in her hand. There was a little boy behind her. He was carrying a heavy load on his head. 'You go home,' she said gently to the boy. 'When you get home, ask Innocent to start cooking. Do you hear?' The boy made for home.

She took my hand. 'You look tired,' she said. I was tired. Very tired.

'Are you set?' I asked.

'Not quite. Mike was packing the children's things when I left for the market. Do you think we are going to run?'

'How do I know? I feel like dying,' I said.

'When I think of Lagos, I cry,' Mike's wife said.

'You shouldn't think of Lagos. Just forget Lagos. You will go mad if you think of Lagos.'

'So this is what it is to be at war? Kate, right from the start I was sceptical about this crisis. You know Mike and I nearly separated. I told our friends, I said please let's not fight. They were shouting and making a lot of noise. I told Mike please let's not leave Lagos. He told me that our marriage was at an end if I did not come with him to the East. You see the suffering. And we have not actually started suffering. Suffering. I have never suffered all my life. You know, I left everything in Enugu. Our house in Lagos, Oh . . .'

'Forget all that, Ifeoma. Are you set in case. Is Mike ready?'

'The two cars are ready,' she said.

'What about petrol?' I asked.

'We bought petrol at black market price.'

'You are set then. We would have given you a gallon if you hadn't. We bought at black market price as well. One pound a gallon. Can you believe it? The government sells at six shillings a gallon. Our people and money. Did you hear of the brigade attack?' I finally asked.

'Brigade attack! There was no brigade attack. Don't mind our people. There was no such thing. They are still deceiving themselves. Nobody is attacking the Nigerians. I am almost sure that they will come. Brigade attack indeed. Why do our people lie so much?' Ifeoma asked.

'They are not lying,' I said. 'They are only boosting our morale.'

'And when they discovered that you were not telling them the truth?' Ifeoma asked.

'They never discovered. They thank you for boosting their morale, and blame saboteurs for showing the enemy the way. Didn't I tell you how a man was nearly beaten to death in Port Harcourt because he said that Asaba had been occupied by the Nigerians. He was telling the truth, but he nearly lost his life. We can't bear the truth.'

'And where will all this lead us to?'

'Heaven knows. I am going. You go home, Ifeoma. You have a long way to go.'

Tears filled her eyes as she turned to go. Tears filled my own eyes. How could this happen to us? Who brought this war on us? Perhaps we were not going to run after all. No, we were going to run. There was no getting out of it.

My husband was angry when I reached home. He had been looking for me. He flared up when I got home. But I was in no mood to quarrel. There was nothing really. He just wanted us to be together. One must be absolutely sure that one was not cut off from one's family.

'Have you tried the car this morning?' I asked him. He shook his head, then got the key and went to the car. For a long time, the car would not start. I went out and watched as he tried to start the car. Then he grew impatient and a bit anxious. 'Try the choke,' I said. He ignored my suggestion got out of the car and opened the bonnet. He readjusted the battery head, touched one or two nuts and tried again. It started and I breathed a sigh of relief. He drove the car to the Lake and up the hill and returned. He then parked it in the garage. Shortly afterwards, we heard the bellman:

'You have all heard, nobody should run. Whether you are a man or woman or child, old and young, you are to remain here. Those who are warming cars in readiness to take flight, are causing panic. There is no danger. The Nigerians are at Omoku. Soon the gallant Biafran forces will drive them out of Omoku.

'All able-bodied men are requested to go the Mission. There are some people from Umuahia who would like to see them. Every able-bodied adult should go there right now. You should take your matchets and knives with you. A set of evil people, infiltrators, were discovered at Osemoto last night. They had maps and coins worth a million pounds. They are at present in the Army camp being interrogated. They were discovered by the security men. That's why we must be vigilant. Those of you who will not go combing, you are all saboteurs. When this war is over you will be dealt with. Those of you who are too big to comb, too big to go to war, you all will be dealt with.' He jingled his bell several times and went on.

The youths whom I met at my aunt's house reached our house. It was the same meaningless consoling words. But this time they had added a big lie which contradicted everything they were saying. There was in fact a brigade attack in Oburuoto the night before. The gallant Biafran forces had wiped out over a battalion of the Nigerian forces. Those who tried to escape had all been drowned. Dead bodies were everywhere, and farmers were being paid three shillings for every Nigerian dead buried. There was no cause for alarm at all. Nigerian soldiers would never set foot on Ugwuta soil.

They went away, my mother-in-law turned and asked me, 'The wife of my son, tell me, how do our people count the dead?' In spite of the tension, my husband and I laughed out aloud.

'No, answer me, I am serious,' my mother-in-law said.

'I must tell you frankly,' I said, 'I don't know. Since this war, I have not seen a battlefield. I have not seen a dead soldier. I have not seen blood. The day I see them, I'll die myself.'

'You have not answered my mother's question,' Chudi said smiling.

'I have said I didn't know,' I said.

'After a battle soldiers charge the forest,' my husband said.

'They don't count the dead when they charge the forest,' I said.

'I haven't said that. Perhaps it is when the forest is charged that they count the dead,' my husband said.

My mother-in-law was not satisfied with these answers.

'We have killed so many Nigerians soldiers, why don't they call off this war? Didn't our people say that there were no young men to fight for Nigeria any more?'

'They are very many, the more we kill the more they come,' Chudi said.

'What do we use to kill them. Not guns. Where do we have ammunition to kill so many at a time?'

'We use *Ogbunigwe*, haven't you heard of it? It kills

49

thousands at a time. It killed over ten thousand at Ugwuoba. Didn't you hear it?'

She was not satisfied with all this. She got up and announced that she was going out. We begged her not to be long, and that if she should hear shooting or anything unusual she should hurry back.

There was nothing one could do other than wait and hope. We were all set. I thought of all sorts of things. Hunger was paramount in my thoughts. Hunger. I have never known hunger all my life. Now I was going to be faced with hunger. My children would be faced with hunger. In a short time they would have kwashiorkor and if we were lucky they might survive, but it could impair their health for life. There was no room in the car for yams. What were we going to eat in the place of our refuge? How long were we going to be there? What would happen if we had no money to eat and nowhere to go?

In packing our things, I had made sure I brought pieces of wrappas I had not cut. There were about five of them. I could sell them to buy food. After selling them, what next? It was unthinkable. It was madness. The war was madness. We were not prepared for this war. We shouldn't have seceded. It was a big miscalculation. I had thought that Gowon was not going to fight us. I had thought that the rest of Nigeria would have been glad to get rid of the Ibos. The Ibos whom they said grabbed all the jobs, all the wealth of the country. The uncivilized Ibos who only the other day had their first lawyer, and who have just had their first generation of doctors and engineers. How dare they rub shoulders with the Yorubas of the West, the civilised whose grandfathers were doctors and lawyers; whose great grandfathers attended Oxford and Cambridge in the last century. How could they dare make a noise and want to be heard in Lagos. Only a few years ago, these same Ibos had come to Lagos to be house-servants and to do the menial jobs. Now they owned properties in Lagos, once owned by their former masters.

No, the Nigerians should not have fought us. We had left Lagos for them. They should have left us in peace in our new found Biafra. We could have built up our Biafra 'where no one would be oppressed'. Was anybody sure of this? 'Where no one would be oppressed'? There was already oppression even before the young nation was able to stand on her feet. Wasn't it even possible that war could have broken out in the young nation if there was no civil war? Perhaps Nigeria did well to attack us. If they hadn't we would have, out of frustration begun to attack and kill one another.

The way the soldiers were carrying on. They were angry, all of them. For what, one was at a loss to determine. They called us the idle civilians. They threatened to shoot at the slightest provocation. What was wrong with them? I kept on asking my husband: 'What was wrong with our soldiers? Why were they behaving in the way they were behaving? But for the civilians Biafra could not have withstood the first phase of the war. It was the civilians who organised 'kitchens' to cook for the soldiers. The lucky soldiers who survived the first battle at Nsukka returned to the base only to discover that there was no food to eat. It was the women, the women alone who organised these 'kitchens.' No, something was wrong somewhere. All was not well.

Exactly ten minutes to twelve noon a shot was heard. It was a heavy shot. It sounded like a rocket. It was similar to the sounds we heard in Port Harcourt before we fled. Instinctively we dived for cover. Then we came out. We thought it was an air-raid. There was no plane in sight. What was it? Then we knew. The Vandals were invading Ugwuta. We were going to run after all.

I got up. I was no longer afraid. My mind was strong. My heart was not beating. I was collected. Where did I de˗˗˗˗ ˗˗˅

strength from? I was ready for action. I could move mountains then. 'Don't panic,' I told my husband. This is the time to pack the suitcases into the car. I called the maid. 'You go and start cooking. The soup is there, so it won't take you time.' I thought of the hundreds of yams in the barn. Even if we returned after forty eight hours, there would be nothing left. Forty eight hours, the war should have ended in forty eight hours.

Our children were playing. I called them in. I told them we were going to leave Ugwuta soon. Anybody who was missing when we were about to leave, would be killed by the Vandals. The eldest who was eight started crying. 'Don't cry,' I consoled . . . 'Look after your sister and brothers.'

'Are we all going in one car?' one of the children asked.

'Yes, all of us, including the big mama.'

'Grandmother will go with us too?' another asked.

'Yes, the big mama is going with us.' I said. 'When the food is ready you will eat'.

I went to the room. Was there anything we were leaving behind that we should take? All had been taken. We had packed for a long time. The children's things were packed two weeks before. We were set. Those things we were not taking with us, we had packed into the ceiling of the house. I remembered Sue saying that there was no point packing those things into the ceiling. What if the house were rocketed? The house could be rocketed, but what was the sense in leaving one's property for the first looter. If he must loot, let the looter do some thinking and some work. There was no sense making things easy for him.

Looting. It was the order of the day. It was our bane. The bane of Biafra. I used to think that only an invading army looted property, not the home army.

I went to see my mother. She told me she was ready. My father had gone for a meeting. He went in the car, otherwise they should have started packing their things into the car.

Unknown to my father, my mother had packed his clothes and sent them to a place she thought was safe. She had a few things and plenty of food. We had some food, and just a few pounds to buy more.

The market was still full, people were still buying and selling. As I was returning I met one of the civil defenders who told me that anybody could buy petrol, that it was being sold at the Mission. I rushed home for a bucket but the queue was so long that I abandoned the idea and returned home.

Then there was another rocketing. The first had exploded at the Naval base, killing an officer. That was enough. That was the advent of the Vandals. That was a warning to civilians to clear out that they were coming. In this respect, they were merciful. But for those rockets many would have died.

At the other end of the mission, the youths were still training. Were they mad? Were they going to face automatic weapons with sticks?

Some villages organised their own youths to defend their own village. They paraded, molesting the women who had already started fleeing. The soldiers had turned many women back. They were merely causing panic.

A young man came up to our house. 'I hear you have already put your things in the car. You are not leaving. We are going to see to it that you don't leave. Nobody will leave. I am not leaving.'

'If you don't leave here now, I'll throw you out. Don't you hear?' Chudi was interrupted by the explosion of a rocket in front of our house. Luckily there was nobody there. My mother-in-law was in sight. Thank God she had not been nearer. The man took to his heels.

The food was ready. We did not eat it. We put it in the car. The maid began to weep. I bundled her into the car. Three of us were in front. My mother-in-law, the maid and the children were in the back.

The car would not start. Luckily, my husband was calm. I was calm too. 'Mother,' I said to my mother-in-law. 'You take the children with you. We shall collect you when the car starts. Just continue walking along the straight road.' My mother-in-law and the children, all burst into tears. My husband ignored them. He was working feverishly on the car.

The naval boys were fleeing. Many were throwing away their uniforms, running up country to Mgbidi and the outskirts, to places of safety.

My mother had taken the children and they were making for Mgbidi as well. A column of women and children had begun to flow past. Children of three were walking to Mgbidi a distance of six miles in the heat of the sun. Then another rocket and yet another.

The car had not started. 'Chudi, try hard. If you abandon it, that's the end,' I told him. I brought water, I brought oil. The human traffic was getting heavier. It was endless. We were in their way and they just swarmed past us like ants. They increased our fear. There was nobody in the market place now. Everybody was moving. The town was moving.

The young man who said he was not budging came along. 'Cowards,' he said. 'Where are you all going? You are all cowards.'

Then a woman, in spite of the heavy load she was carrying addressed him: 'Aniche, a goat sucked your mother's breast. Poor fool. What happened to your father will happen to you. Senseless fool. Hopeless idiot. You stay and be killed by the Nigerians. Don't you see all Ugwuta evacuating? "Onye Afufu" stay and die.'

Aniche did not even hear her. He went on. I was becoming frantic. My husband was becoming frantic, too. Another rocket had exploded a few yards away. There was a man running towards us. He was hefty. Chudi recognised him as a driver at the naval base. He called him. He stopped as he saw it was my husband and me.

'The car will not start,' Chudi said plaintively.

'Get in,' he said. 'Get in quickly. They are here. I saw their boat on the Lake.' He tried to start the car. It wouldn't start. He jumped out. 'Pull the bonnet release,' he said urgently. My husband pulled it. He opened the bonnet. He touched a nut here and a nut there. 'I see. We are all right.' He jumped in and the car started. We drove forward. Women and children waved at us, but we did not stop.

There was a bus by the side of the road with no driver. There were boxes and property of all kinds. They were abandoned. The owners had taken flight.

My husband remembered his sister. We must go to their house to see if they had left. Fortunately, they had left. Their door was locked. I smiled, remembering that I asked her not to lock the door. We left ours ajar, so that they did not break it, and thus avoid expenses of repairing the doors and the locks if we ever came back. There was always hope that we would come back. It was just for a little while. It didn't occur to us that we would never come back to a place taken by the Nigerians. When they came, they dug in with the help of their superior weapons.

Those waiting to collect petrol had abandoned their containers and fled as the rockets exploded more and more frequently. I knew the petrol would be abandoned to the enemy. Why, why did they not give petrol to people who wanted it a week before? They did not do it because they said that those who had cars would run away and cause panic. The people who took this decision all had cars!

The exodus from Ugwuta continued. My God, so there were so many people in Ugwuta! Old and young, men and women and children. Goats and sheep. They were walking, walking out of Ugwuta to an unknown destination. Soon, perhaps the buildings and the trees would develop legs and begin to walk. No it was not possible. It could not be possible.

Everything that was happening in Biafra then was impossible. The rockets were falling, indiscriminately. We had now collected my mother-in-law and the children and had climbed out of rocket range because our mother complained that the soup was pouring away.

I sat down near the road. People were passing. Children were crying: Women were crying: 'Uhamiri, why have you treated us in this way? The Woman of the Lake, the thunderer, the hairy woman. The most beautiful woman in the world. The ageless woman. Why, why have you done this to your children? Did we not sacrifice to you? Did we not keep holy your holy day? Did we not worship you with our whole heart? Why have you brought this death on us?'

They wept as they went. Where were they going? None of them knew. They knew only that they were going to a place of safety, away from the rockets, away from guns, away from this madness, this fearful insanity.

Vehicles were going back. Perhaps to collect one or two more things. Then I saw Pat. He had a brand new Peugeot car. He was confused. 'Kate, where is my wife?' and before I answered, 'Where are my children?'

'You fool,' my mother-in-law shouted. 'You big fool. You left Ugwuta this morning without making preparation for your wife and children. You and your wife nearly deceived me. Look for your wife and children. We don't know where they are.'

'They had left the house before we left,' I said. 'Chudi went there. They must be nearing Mgbidi by now. Never mind. They left quite early.'

'Thank God', he breathed a sigh of relief. My God! Christ! My briefcase. My briefcase is in the house. I must go and take it.'

'Over my dead body. If you go you will not come back', my mother-in-law said. 'Look at the fool saying he would go back to Ugwuta. Look, their boats were seen before we fled.

56

They have occupied the whole place now.'

Then a car stopped. Pat went near and asked the driver: 'Are they in Ugwuta?' The driver shook his head. He was very sad.

'So they have entered?'

'They have landed. I couldn't go in. The Rev. Father is there turning back people wanting to go in. The last people who went in were still there. It is feared that they had met with the Vandals. That means death. The Rev. Father saw them himself. There were white mercenaries with them. The Rev. Father saw a man shot by the Vandals. The man was running; he was shot and he fell.'

We had not driven half a mile when we saw a group of wome surrounding some object on the ground. My husband stopped the car. My mother-in-law came out first. I was still in the car, but when she shouted, I rushed out.

It was a pregnant woman. She could not walk any more. The baby in her womb was rebellious. It was kicking and kicking. And the kicking was visible on her protruding stomach. She lay there unable to get up and walk. Her children were there. They were crying. 'Mother please, please mother. Don't have the baby here. Not here mother. Not today. Today is a bad day.'

The baby kept on kicking. It did not hear the pleadings of the children. The women did not know what to do. It was not time. But perhaps she would have a premature baby.

'How do you feel?' my mother-in-law asked. She merely shook her head. 'My husband, he is not here. He refused to leave. I left with the children. Perhaps he has been killed by the Nigerians. Oh!!' she gave out an agonizing shout. 'I am going to have it. It is actual labour now. I feel the baby is coming out. Oh, my God. Mama, call my mother. Call her. Call her . . .'

Her mother had died years ago. 'He refused to come with us. I begged him to come. He refused. I am without a husband.'

'Mama, he will come. He will. Don't worry,' one of her daughters pleaded.

'You should not be crying like this,' my mother-in-law said.

'Mama, I am without a husband. My husband has been killed by the Nigerians. He is a strong headed husband. He refused to leave with us. I begged him. No, No. It has come again. It has come again. Again, hold me, it's coming. I am going to die. Mama I'll die, I am going to die. To die, to die to die.... my...' She was dead.

We stood there and looked from the corpse to the children. At first they did not understand. It was the eldest who first realised what had happened. She threw herself on the ground and yelled and yelled.

We stood. Others joined us. We watched. Then a rocket, another, and yet another. We took cover. We lay on our stomachs. The body was peaceful. It had no need to take cover. She was at peace with her God. God had ended her suffering. She would no longer suffer.

'They are coming. Move on. They are marching to the airstrip.' It was the good Rev. Gentleman. 'Off you go.' Then he saw. He stopped. 'Run along all of you. I'll bury her. I'll give her the last sacrament.' He did. I couldn't go. That was the first dead body I saw during the war. The woman who had spoken a few minutes ago was a corpse. Was death so quick? Was it as quick as it was cruel? What was the cause of death?

'Kate, are you mad? Don't you hear the rockets?' Chudi's harsh voice roused me. The children were crying in the car. There was a stampede as women threw away their loads to take cover. God, spare us this madness. This insanity, this hell on earth. This sudden darkness. This end of the world. A whole town moving. The buildings would begin to move in a short time. Yes, why not. The aged were moving. They were moving corpses, with sticks, with walking sticks, skeletons.

In a day or two they would die like the pregnant woman. And nobody would bury them. They would rot and decay and mingle with mother earth. Then, their bones would remain. No! Life was cruel. Life was meaningless. Was there no purpose, nothing? Just emptiness? The war. Who caused the war? The Woman of the Lake, why, why, why did you allow this to happen to your children? We have sinned. All of us have sinned against the Woman of the Lake, against the gods and goddesses of the land. We were all guilty. But the punishment is too great, too severe, too crude, too raw for our offences against the gods, the great woman. The Holy Spirit. Yes that. The sin against the Holy Spirit will not be forgiven, so the Scriptures say. What is the sin against the Holy Spirit? I do not understand. The world is a strange and mysterious place . . .

There were more and more corpses as we moved along. I shut my eyes. We moved on. We moved on for fear that if we did not move on we might be corpses ourselves. We moved on along the tarred road. The road that was built barely three years before the crisis. The political road, so we called it in those good old days. So those days could be referred to as good old days. Only the other day we rejoiced in the streets at the arrival of the soldiers. I particularly believed in a benevolent dictatorship. Someone told me I did not know what I was talking about. There was no such thing as a benevolent dictatorship. Not with human beings. It could be possible with gods.

We arrived at Mgbidi. It was only six miles away from Ugwuta. There was peace. There was life. They hadn't the slightest notion of what we had gone through. They did not know that the enemy was six miles away, that they had occupied Ugwuta. They should, they could take Uli airstrip that night if they wanted to. Nobody would stop them. Why don't they tell them to march on and march on, so that, this madness will end. So the war will end. The war end in our life time? Biafrans won't give in. Biafrans won't surrender. Surrender and die? They will die to the last man.

At Mgbidi petrol was being sold. We filled our tank. What next, where do we go? Men and woman, old and young sat on both sides of the road homeless, comfortless. The sun was intense. Thank God for the tropical sun. Thank God for all His mercies. He sent us the sun on a day like this. Thank Him that He did not send us rain. Rain would have destroyed all our things. Many have begun to move. Where were they moving to? Towards Owerri? Owerri was in imminent danger.

We didn't know what to do next. We sat there with the others, a sea of human beings. I thought of home, then suddenly someone spoke. I got up. 'Ugwuta is on fire. Ugwuta is being burnt. We are lost.' Yes, true enough Ugwuta, the land of our ancestors was on fire. We saw the smoke. The Vandals had set fire to Ugwuta. How sad. How very sad. There was no return. The women wept. Some of the men wept. The smoke was heavy. We could see it six miles away. Our home was six miles away. The Vandals had occupied it. How long were we going to be refugees? Would we be able to return to Ugwuta in our lifetime? No we were merely dreaming. We would wake up one morning to discover that all that had happened was a dream.

'Ugwuta Ameshi, *Ugwuta Ameshi e e* Are you there? Is Uhamiri there? Do you see? Sabo, you have done your worst. I am a dead woman. I am a dead and wretched woman. My God, my people, have you seen my nakedness? Uhamiri, you have not done well. You have not done well at all . . .' 'It is enough, it is enough. Ewoo, what kind of thing is this?'

It was no other than the woman politician Madam Agafa. She was surrounded by women, the prayer group. She was sweating profusely, and some women were fanning her.

Most of the women were in tears as Madam Agafa wept and called upon the Woman of the Lake to save her people.

Then my mother-in-law came. 'What are you all doing here weeping? You have not started to weep. You will weep for a long time to come. Agafa get up, get up. Why do you stay here allowing all these women to weep on you? Are you insane? Have you gone out of your mind? Why are you behaving like a child? Get up quickly I say. We are all alive. We shall pick up again.'

'Uberife, Uberife, Uberife, you have spoken well.' Madam Agafa spoke in between sobs. I went to Owerri this morning. They assured me everything was all right. That man, that head of the Navy, I went to him last night. I told him I was afraid. Was it necessary for us to evacuate? He laughed at me. He said I was a coward. He took me to a place were he showed me all the arms and ammunition. He said it would be suicidal for the Nigerians to make an attempt. I was deceived. I was deceived by my people. I left Ugwuta this morning. Did you see any of my children? Where are my children?'

'Your children are safe. They will soon be here. Your brother took them. I saw them. They took the Egbu road. They said they were making for the farm. Wipe your tears. Wipe your tears. Your children are safe.'

'Mama, we have told her they are safe. But she does not want to hear. She does not believe us.'

'They have told me. Uberife, they have told me. I came to the world empty-handed, naked. I am going back empty-handed. Ewoo, my God. Gowon, you have done your worst. Gowon, Gowon, have you seen? Have you seen what you have caused? Gowon, I say you have done your worst.

'You are crazy, Agafa you are crazy. Leave her to talk like a woman possessed.' My mother-in-law left the crowd of women.

What next? Where do we go? Mgbibi people were nowhere

to be found. One or two of them came round, shook their heads and disappeared. Then a bold one came up. He was on his bicycle. It was an old bicycle. He kept on shouting. 'Sabo, Sabo, Sabo. Why are you running? Sabo. Why, why are you running? Go back to your lake. Go back, go back to Uhamiri. You are not Ibos. You say you are not Ibos. Sabo. Sabo. You have allowed Nigerians to enter your town and you are running away. Sabo. All of you are Sabo. Everyone of you. Everyone of you here. Sabo. Sabo.'

'Hee, hee, that man shut your mouth.' I turned, it was Ezekoro. Poor mad Ezekoro. So he had joined us as well. Poor miserable mad man. He would die a refugee. Ezekoro was a mad man. For several years, he was deaf and dumb. Then miraculously he regained his speech, and he talked and talked and talked.

'Shut up,' Ezekoro said. 'You have killed Ugwuta. You, you murdered Ugwuta. The whole lot of you. All of you. You murdered Enugu, you murdered Onitsha, you murdered Port Harcourt. And now Ugwuta. You, you, you and all your people. All your people. But let me tell you, you can't murder Ugwuta. You cannot. I am going back to Ugwuta to save her. I will save Ugwuta. Nobody will save her but me. Dirty Nigerians, they can't fight. I'll drive them away with my fan.' He waved his fan above his head, then made for Ugwuta. Nobody could stop him. He made for his death, certain death. Nobody saw him again.

'You must move now, everyone of you start moving. The next thing will be an air-raid. I know the Nigerians. I know them too well.' That was the good Reverend gentleman. He was always organising, always doing good, always positive in his actions. How he hated and loved us all at once. Yes, he hated and loved the Biafrans. He had worked with us for over thirty years. He knew us and more. He said he would die for the cause. He had escaped death many times. He had been captured once by the Nigerian troops and sent to

Lagos, then to Rome. He came back to Biafra to continue the good work.

May the Almighty God be blessed. There was no air-raid. There was no rain. Only the sun. 'Keep clear of the roads', he advised. 'Go into the bush, right into the bush. It will be all right.'

One or two cars passed. They did not stop. Only the Army officers drove cars these days. Then one came. It stopped. It was a white man. A mercenary. Where is Agnes? He must be French. No, either Italian or French. Agnes was trained in the Congo, Kinshasa they call it now. Where is she? I saw her a moment ago. I looked round and asked one of the children to look for Agnes. He went in search of her. The white man was nearly six foot tall. He had a beard. He smiled as he saw us. He gesticulated. We smiled back. 'We speak English', I said. He laughed. He understood. 'I speak a little English.' He said with difficulty. 'The Nigerians, they are here. No, in Ugwuta, no Oguta. There. Six miles inside. Water. By the lake from Port Harcourt,' Chudi was trying to communicate. The mercenary smiled again. Then as luck would have it, Agnes came. She spoke French as she had never spoken before. We were at a loss. We did not understand.

Agnes was beaming with smiles. The mercenary was unperturbed. 'Tell us, Agnes, what does he think about it all? Will the Biafran forces attack tonight? If they don't attack, that will be the end of us. The end of the war. The Uli airstrip is not very far away. They can take it in a matter of hours if nothing is done to-night. This very night,' Chudi said.

Agnes interpreted. The mercenary said he was on his way to Umuahia. And that the Vandals would be wiped out in a matter of hours. 'Ask him, ask him to send his men to night. They must attack to night. If not, we are finished. The war is over,' I said. Agnes interpreted again. The mercenary smiled again. He went into his car. He was travelling alone. I wondered why they let them travel alone.

63

Then Agnes went in as well. Then she waved to us. Further down the road, the car stopped. Agnes jumped out. She collected her suitcase and that of her younger sister. She gave some money to her mother and father and asked her sister to come with her. They drove away. The Mercenary had captured a Biafran girl. No, two Biafran girls. What else could she do. I mean Agnes. She had no money. She had nowhere to go but to the farm. She had never been to the farm since she was born. Poor girl. She had just graduated when the crisis came. She returned. And she continued blaming herself for returning when she did. She had made several attempts to go back, but was unable. At one time in Port Harcourt she had actually gone to the airport to take her plane, but was sadly disappointed. She then resigned herself to fate. Perhaps the Mercenary would take her to France.

'Haven't you heard?' somebody was saying. 'They are marching to the air strip. They must take the airstrip tonight. What was the purpose of invading if not to take the Uli airstrip?'

He was right. We took the road to Akatta. That was the place we decided to go. My father decided on that place. Some people went to Ihiala, others to Okija and others to Owerri. Some crossed the Urashi River to the farm. About three quarters of Ugwuta people went to the farm by this route.

We drove to Akatta. It was a rough road. The children were all tired and hungry. The younger ones began to cry. I consoled them. Chudi drove on. It was getting dark now. There were so many check points on the road. Every village we came to called us saboteurs and refused to let us pass. We had allowed the Nigerians to take our town, we were all saboteurs. We all deserved to be shot, just as the original

64

saboteurs were shot. My blood ran cold. I knew the original saboteurs. I didn't know why they were shot. God pardon Biafra. Forgive this blindness, this folly.

Many Ugwuta people tried to explain. Nobody would listen. Many slept on the road. Many were refused accommodation on the school premises. It was painful. We drove on. Then we came to the cross roads. We took the left turn. It was a winding road. We saw the sign board which indicated where we were going. We stopped the car. My parents and the children were all there. The children were running about. Did they think they were on holiday or what?

We unpacked quietly. My mother and my mother-in-law were weeping. My father was upstairs lying down. (The landlord had given us a large apartment upstairs.) When he saw me he got up from the bed. He pointed to the next room. We put our things there. Then we went downstairs. After some time, it was completely dark.

The landlord came in. He was a young man of about thirty eight. He had known my father at Aba where he traded. When the war broke out, he acted quickly. First, he took home his wife and children, then he completed the village house he was building, then in December, 1967, he finally returned home. But he occasionally went to Aba to do some business. He had prepared himself for a really rough time.

The problem of water worried him. So he bought huge tanks. But those were for the rainy season. The dry season was really hard. The stream was six miles away.

He greeted us warmly. It was obvious that he was a bit uncomfortable. He had not expected to see so many people. My parents came with a battalion of children. There were six children of my late uncle, then my uncle who had three wives came with fifteen children. My brother who had just been married had his wife and a young son of eighteen months, and his wife was now expecting another baby. I came with my husband, mother-in-law and our children. There was my aunt who was a widow, and she came with three children. The others were dependants and maids. They numbered eight.

That night, Chudi and my brother slept in the car. Some children slept outside. It was a miserable sight, we were awake until about one in the morning. The landlord kept assuring us there was no danger. The Nigerians were not in Ugwuta, Radio Biafra had said that the enemy had been in Omoku, but they had been wiped out. In fact, in a short time, the gallant Biafran forces would enter Port Harcourt.

He was so sure of his information that I thought that we had all gone mad.

'I tell you,' he said, 'and I say mark my words, the Biafran forces will be in Port Harcourt in a matter of days. Mark my words. Just quote me.' As if quoting him would make it more true.

'But there had been shelling for days and rocketing today,' I said gently knowing that we were at his mercy, for that night at least.

'Ahaa, that's nothing. Nothing at all. Only *sabos* were causing the trouble.'

'And the driver who made my car start said he saw them on the Lake with his own eyes,' Chudi ventured.

'He is a saboteur,' the landlord declared. 'He wanted to loot your property, why didn't you hand him over to the Army?' 'There was no army. They fled before the civilians,' I retorted.

There was no point discussing with him. He had all the answers. He was so sure of himself. He knew everybody in Biafra. All the Brigadiers and Colonels and Lt. Colonels were his personal friends. The majors and captains were small fry.

He tuned into all the stations on his radio to get the latest news. He kept awake trying to tune into the stations that he thought would carry news of the war.

What really worried us that night was the airstrip. There was shooting throughout the night as planes attempted to land. At Ugwuta we did not sleep properly if we did not hear planes at night because that meant that arms and ammunition were not coming in. But when there were planes, we woke up greatly relieved, and dared the Nigerians to continue their war of aggression on a young progressive Biafra.

We snatched a little sleep. In the morning we woke up to the realisation of where we were. We were surrounded by very thick and tall trees. They all stood solidly silently, aggressively, as if they dared us to approach. There were palm trees as well and palm raffia very much like palm trees. The soil was dry, infertile and hungry. There did not seem to be any life on it. The cassava shrubs were thin and tender and sick looking. There was evidence that they hadn't grown bigger since the previous year.

How long were we going to be here? I kept thinking. How long? I felt some thing crawling on my hands. When I examined them closely I found swellings from almost invisible insects. I slapped promptly, killing several of them. There were swellings all over my hands. In a short time I would suffer from craw-craw. My God! Craw-craw! I, suffer from craw-craw.

There were no vegetables of any kind. The *Ugu* vegetables had withered long ago. It was September. What a land. What were we going to eat? How long would our food last?

The children of the landlord were quite healthy, well, as healthy as they could be at the time. There were about eight of them, and their mother was expecting another one. The eldest was barely ten years old.

The house was quite spacious, though it could not take all of us. What we had to do was look for another accommodation. There were too many of us.

The landlord brought my father a pot of fresh palm wine. It was the best palm wine I had ever tasted in all my life. I had two glasses and wanted another, but refrained from asking for more for fear that I would be accused of being greedy.

We prepared breakfast. The standard of our breakfast fell. That was the first morning. What would the following mornings, endless mornings, look like? It was difficult to imagine.

The landlord had left as soon as he brought the palm wine. He had some business in town, some twelve miles away. He went on his bicycle. He had talked to my father that morning. We did not know what they talked about.

The children stared at us as we ate. Didn't they have their own breakfast? Their mother had gone to the farm without giving them anything to eat. Was this usual? Didn't they eat in the mornings?

After breakfast, what next? What next? We had to live. We just had to survive. We should get decent accommodation first. That was the first priority. The landlord had said that accommodation was easy. He had so many relations in the village who had zinc houses. If it were a zinc house, it was all right.

My husband and I went in search of a zinc house, while my mother and mother-in-law went to the market to see what could be bought. The car was so small we took only a few yams. We needed food, but we had very little money.

We went in search of accommodation. There were far too many people. Soon there would be grumblings over so many things especially over food. Which pot could cook all the food? It would be easier to get accommodation elsewhere. It was not easy for one to live with one's parents after marriage. Living with one's mother-in-law was worse.

The path was very narrow, the trees tall. There were few palm trees. The little girl who was our guide walked so fast we could hardly keep up. She knew the intricate paths, the entanglements and the nooks and corners. By the time we got to the house, we were exhausted.

Luckily, the landlord was there. He welcomed us very well, and showed us the two rooms he had reserved for us. They were of course empty. It was a zinc house. The floor was cemented. He showed us the kitchen. It was the same kitchen his wife used. I wondered how we were going to share one kitchen. Two women, sharing one kitchen. It was not easy.

We told him we would have it. That we were going to bring our things in the evening.

Coming back, we saw the poverty of the people staring us in the face. There was barrenness everywhere. The people had only their palm wine and nothing else. The children we saw looked ill. There was visible sign of kwashiorkor in them. In a short time, they would all suffer from the deadly disease, one of the banes of Biafra. There was no getting out of it, unless something was done.

On our way back, I kept asking Chudi how long he thought we would be in Akatta. It was a God-forsaken place. There was no life. There was no water. And when we had no food, what would happen? He kept saying consolingly, never mind, something would happen. Perhaps Ugwuta would be cleared, and we shall go back.

'Tell me where that has been possible?' I retorted.

'Never mind,' he said. 'This might be an exception. You never can tell.' Really I began to hope again.

My mother and mother-in-law came back from the market with plenty of food. The price of foodstuffs had risen by a hundred percent since the fall of Ugwuta. Ugwuta fed the whole of Mgbidi division and the environs. Now Ugwuta had fallen. Where would the people buy food? Fish, cassava, yams, plantains etc. came from Ugwuta. What next?

Water. The tanks were filled with water. But none of us had a wash that morning. How could we when water had to be saved? It was the rainy season all right, but one was not sure what to expect. The children had not taken kindly to this at all. They were used to having their baths first thing in the morning. The tap ran twenty four hours. Now, they had to forgo their baths. Fancy economising on water of all things. The children kept on asking when they could have their baths. My mother told them they could when it rained.

Fortunately, it did rain that afternoon. The children filled all the containers they could find and had their baths. It reminded me of school. The stream was nearly six miles away. But if it rained at night or in the day, we filled everything including our food bowls and drinking cups.

We did not go out in the evening. My father would not let us. If we must all die, let's all die together. That was my father. But I did not like the sentiment. I told him we were only in the neighbourhood. If we stayed apart, a little apart, we would be more able to take the hardship and maintain good relationship. I knew that in a short time when money began to run out, we would be on edge. There were signs of it already. However we stayed another night.

My brother had gone to Mgbidi to hunt for news. He came back with an unbelievable news. Ugwuta had been cleared! Ugwuta had been cleared! No, we couldn't believe it. I couldn't believe it. It was too good to be true. It was big news, mighty news. We could not swallow it. Yet we rejoiced. We sang the Biafran national anthem. I never knew the words. But the tune was fantastic. There was a kind of awe it provoked in us. It was the tune that reminded one of one's surpreme sacrifice. We had all, from all corners of Nigeria converged at our home, not because of oppression, nobody was oppressed, but because of fear for our lives. One did not just desert one's job, one's home, and more, one's friends, for fun.

No, it was not possible. 'Tell us what had happened,' I said to my brother.

'Simple. The gallant Biafran forces had retaken Ugwuta in less than forty eight hours.'

'You are lying,' That was my mother. My brother ignored her, though he was hurt. He went to our father. 'We want to go to Ugwuta. I saw people going to Ugwuta. Give me the car please.'

'You wait a bit,' Papa said. 'It is already late. You will go in the morning. I cannot believe it though. Wait until morning.'

Nobody slept that night. The landlord was the chief information officer. His information was what he had already told us, that Ugwuta had not fallen at all. No news media carried the news of the clearance. Radio Biafra of course did. That meant that it accepted the fact that Ugwuta had fallen.

That night also, planes landed. I did not know how many but they landed and took off. It was true then that Ugwuta had been cleared. Planes could not land or take off in Uli when the federal troops were in Ugwuta. It was impossible.

The next morning, I accompanied Chudi and brother to Mgbidi. There was a big road block. There were so many people. Nobody was allowed to go in. The check point was full of soldiers in battle dress. They looked wretched and hungry. There were no officers.

They joined the crowd in waiting. How did it happen? There were different versions of the story. The people who were at Mgbidi swore that they saw Ojukwu and two mercenaries plan the attack at the junction of Ugwuta-Owerri road. The map of Ugwuta was brought to them and they, after studying it, planned and led the attack themselves. One or two people even said that Ojukwu was wounded in the attack. The women wept when they heard that their leader was wounded.

Nobody knew for certain how it all happened. All that they knew and appreciated was that the Federal troops had been driven out from Ugwuta and that they were waiting to re-enter their home. The Woman of the Lake had not after all let them down.

A car was approaching from Ugwuta at top speed. The people made way. The stick of the check-point was lowered. A gruffy looking Biafran Officer jumped out as the car screeched to a halt.

'We have done it,' he said, raising his fist in acknowledgement of the wave of cheers that greeted him.

'Thank you, my son,' cheered the elderly women.

'When can we go back?' an aged woman asked.

'Not yet, mama, we have to have Ugwuta thoroughly combed first.'

'What about our property, is it safe?'

'Who talks about property?' the officer roared. 'You should be happy that you have the land. It cost blood, you know. As for property, soldiers loot everywhere.'

Somebody said, 'If the Nigerians loot, it's understandable. But why should we loot? It is unbiafran.'

'That's all very well. But remember we are a starving army. We loot to eat. OK? Remember too, the spirit of Biafra is: our land first. Give us somewhere to stand and we'll move the world.' He jerked open the car door went in and banged the door shut. Leaning out of the window, he said, 'When you go back to Ugwuta, think not of your property but of the blood we spilled to set it free. Build anew, that's what Biafra means. Driver, move!'

More cars streamed past. Some were actually loaded with looted property. Jubilant soldiers were shooting random bursts from their guns amidst shouts of: 'Vandals done crape! Fish done chop them!'

Nobody was allowed into Ugwuta until late in the afternoon. We first drove to our house. There were bullet wounds all over the walls. We did not linger. There were still soldiers, real soldiers who were still in tattered battle dress

72

on the streets. They had their guns and looked formidable.

We picked up some cooking pots and pans. The barn was intact. We selected very large yams, as much as we could take in the car. There was a bucket we had dropped when we were fleeing. We collected that as well. The goat and sheep had disappeared; a loss that made my mother-in-law weep. The goat was pregnant. It was a goat that usually had quadruplets.

At my father's house, my brother collected his radio, record player and his wife's box which they left behind in their hurry. There were no bullet marks on the walls. The bags of rice, tins of palm oil and groundnut oil left at the door step had all disappeared. We were looking round to see whether they could get one or two useful items when we heard a gun shot. It was a distant shot but we jumped into the car and drove off. Apart from some few soldiers on the streets, Ugwuta was desolate and empty. Only a few days before, the place was swarming with people. Now it was empty. It was a battle ground. Where were the Nigerian troops who entered it barely three days ago? Where was everybody? What folly! What arrogance, what stupidity led us to this desolation, to this madness, to this wickedness, to this war, to this death? When this cruel war was over, there will be no more war. It will not happen again, never again. NEVER AGAIN, never again.

Why, we were all brothers, we were all colleagues, all friends, all contemporaries, then, without warning, they began to shoot, without warning, they began to plunder and to loot and to rape and to desecrate and more, to lie, to lie against one another. What was secret was proclaimed on the house tops. What was holy was desecrated and abused. NEVER AGAIN.

There was a check point before Mgbidi. It was not there when we passed barely thirty minutes earlier. A rough soldier came along. 'Open your boot. So we won't eat. Bring them all out. All of them.' He meant the yams. The driver hesitated. 'Bring them out quickly I say.'

Chudi and brother jumped out of the car. 'Do what you are told,' my brother said to the driver. The driver began, painfully to bring out the yams from the boot. He deliberately left three.

'All of them,' the soldier said.

'Leave those for us, we too must eat,' that was Chudi.

'You idle civilian, if you don't shut up, I'll finish you. True to God, I'll finish you.'

All the yams came out. Another soldier came along, and got hold of the radio. 'I gonna keep this, eh . . . Ye man, I gonna keep this.'

My brother looked at him: 'Hee, you, of course it is you. It can't be anyone else.'

'Hee, what's cracking?' the soldier raised his head. Thank God there was a sign of recognition on the soldier's face. Thank God he still had some humanity, he was still human, all had not gone with the wind.

'So you did this marvellous job. This is my home, you know.' That was my brother again. 'Where is your uncle?' he continued. The soldier said nothing. He simply turned to the driver and said quietly, 'Put the yams back.'

His comrade turned: 'What say you, eh?'

'I said, put the yams back. Don't molest them. Leave them to go.' The yams were put back into the boot.

Thankfully, we drove off. 'That was the boy I taught barely two years ago. He dropped out in class four. Thank God he recognised me. We would have gone away empty-handed. They could have commandeered the car. He was one of the worst pupils I had ever taught. He was a thief and a dirty liar. While at school, there was no evil he did not excel in. Now he is a soldier, not even an officer. His uncle told me he had joined the army, this was before Enugu fell. And up till now he is not an officer. He had not distinguished himself

74

even in battle. He has always been a ne'er do well.'

At Mgbidi we met many more Ugwuta people who were not allowed to enter their homes. We were let in because we happened to know who was at the checkpoint at the time. So the people thronged round us. 'So it is true?' one of the women asked.

'It is perfectly true, don't you see the boot of our car? It is true, the gallant Biafran forces have done it again. They have wiped out the Vandals.'

'Did you get to the Lake?' One of the men asked.

'No, we didn't get to the Lake. We had no business there.'

'So we can go back to Ugwuta in a day or two?'

'Of course,' my brother said. He was becoming a chief information officer.

The people rejoiced. Long live Biafra, long live Ojukwu. Didn't Ojukwu assure them that nothing would happen to Ugwuta, that he was going to defend every inch of Ugwuta. He had kept his word. They dared the Vandals to come. They dared Gowon to continue his war of aggression on the peace-loving people of Biafra. They were now prepared to fight, to starve and to die for Biafra.

Only a short while before, some hen-pecked men from Ugwuta had gathered in Mgbidi to find out whether there was any possibility of seeing Ojukwu so that he could end the war. Now they were ready to die because their homeland had been saved.

There were no longer check-points as we drove to Akatta. The news of the clearance of the Vandals from Ugwuta had spread like wildfire.

All sorts of rumours had been flying around during our absence from Akatta. One had been rather disturbing. It was strongly rumoured that great havoc had been done by the Vandals. They did not only set the town on fire, they did not only loot but they killed as well. My aunt who had refused to leave had been killed. This latter was true because her

75

husband had come to the house when we were away. He had refused to eat or drink. His wife was dead. When he would not be consoled, almost everybody had joined him. By the time we were back the whole house was one chant of bitter weeping and heavy sighing. Our return was like sunshine in a cloudy day.

'Are you sure they are no longer in Ugwuta,' they asked.

'They are not,' I replied.

'They are there. They killed my wife. They shot her on the arm, and she bled to death.' It was the first time since he came, that the old man had told us how his wife died.

'She was stubborn,' he continued. 'My wife had always been stubborn. It was the will of God. It was the will of the Woman of the Lake that she should end that way. The gods have willed it. Their will must be done. It was so written.' There were tears in his eyes. He was in his sixties. He still had tears in his aged eyes. 'They killed my precious wife. The beautiful Ona. They killed her. Shot her. When we heard their gun shot, we took to our heels. I was faster. Before she could hide, a soldier shot her. He shot her in her arm. Ona's beautiful arm. She shouted as she fell, "My husband, they have killed me." Can I live down those last words of my wife? My husband they have killed me, I got up boldly from where I was hiding, and dragged her limp body to my hiding place. There were more shootings. She was still breathing. In spite of the shooting I laid her down gently, opened a side door behind the house and made for the doctor. I did not see a soul as I went to bring the doctor. There was no one when I got there. Where were the people? So Ugwuta people had all gone. Where did the whole town go? I couldn't believe it. A few days ago the place was teeming with people. The people bought and sold. The children played in the streets. Goats and chickens were roaming the place. Now there was no living thing. I was the only man living in Ugwuta.

'There was another shot. I hid among the trees. I was not

the only one. The enemy was there as well. The Hausas were in Ugwuta. So only the Hausas and I were the occupants of Ugwuta.

'The doctor was not there. A fool. I was a fool. I shouldn't have given in to her. I should have carried her forcibly when she insisted on remaining behind when others had fled. Oh, it was that man, that son of a bitch. He did it. He and his gang told us to remain behind. They said they were going to fight the Vandals. They encouraged us to remain behind and die. They killed my wife. They killed Ona. The blood of Ona will be on their heads. God, don't forgive them. My ancestors, don't forgive them. Because they killed my wife.'

We allowed him to talk. We thought it would do him good if we let him talk. 'The doctor had fled. I had to go back to Ona. She was lying there, lonely. I touched her. She was still breathing. I couldn't leave her there to die lonely. She was still bleeding. How could I stop the bleeding? How, how could I stop it. Yes, I know. I tore one of her wrappas and tied her arm as hard as my strength would let me. She made no sign of pain. If only I could find help. I got up, and peeped through the hole at the door. There was nobody. I could hear movements. I could hear boots on the floor of Okwosha's house. They were military boots. They were soldiers, Vandals who had come to plunder and to loot. God in heaven help us. I saw my wife dying. I was helpless. Ona was dying bfore my very eyes.

'Ona died. I laid her down again gently. Her head had been on my lap all the time. There was gun shot in the distance. That was for Ona. I got up. There was nothing else to be done. She was dead. I had to get out.

'It was getting very dark. I knew of a path which I could take without being seen. Silently and sorrowfully I took the path. There was no soul seen as I made my way through the bush path to Awo-Omama. I did not hear any more gun shots. It was pitch dark now. I got to a huge tree. I lay down there waiting for morning.

'Morning came. Morning without Ona. I walked to the road. I saw a check point. There were some soldiers there. They could be Nigerian soldiers. I hid. Then after sometime, I summoned up courage. Ona was dead, what else was left for me in the world? They were our soldiers, Biafran soldiers. They did not molest me.

'You did not come out?' one of them asked me. No, I did not come out. My wife did not come out. She was shot. Her dead body was at the back of our house. They must have taken me to be a mad man. They let me go. And here I am, Kate's mother.' He turned to my mother. That was what he always called her. 'Kate's mother, my wife is dead. Your sister is dead.' He burst into tears again. We couldn't help weeping too. And once more the chant of weeping rent the air.

My father took him to his room. He gave him a change of clothes. We sat there, happy that Ugwuta had been cleared, sad that so many lives had been lost.

Another death was that of Aniche. He had refused to run. He had called those who fled cowards. He was a hefty man. Must have been twenty seven or less. When he heard the shooting, he hid in the barn. But his senseless mother who was equally stubborn called him to the house to look after his children. His wife had gone to the attack trade. He was in the room, the Vandals entered. He hid behind the door. The Vandals saw his legs. A fool he was. They dragged him out.

'Who are you?' He said not a word. 'Who are you?' He had lost his speech. They beat him, threw him down and used their boot on him. Then they dragged him out, and took him to a house near the Lake where they kept the prisoners. He died there. His mother and children they took as well to the house. They did not beat them but locked them up with the other prisoners.

There was another woman who was shot in front of her

house. Poor woman. She was stone deaf. She refused to leave. When the Nigerian troops advanced, she rushed out of her house, and shouted, 'Long live Biafra, long live Ojukwu!' A Nigerian soldier shot her quickly to quieten her.

In the house where the Nigerian soldiers made their prison were all sorts of men including vagabonds and mad men. They gave them food to eat. One of the old women had the privilege of having her photograph taken by a white mercenary. She was asked whether she had children. She said she had no children. Actually she had four children who pleaded with her to come with them but she refused. Then there was a couple who were ordered out of the prison by the Federal troops because they were noisy. They sent them back to their house with a soldier to keep guard. The man had, since their arrival at the prison camp constantly nagged his wife for failing to bring his pipe and tobacco for him.

The next morning, we heard the shocking news that Owerri had fallen. We found it hard to believe.

'No, it can't be true,' Chudi said. 'Owerri can't fall. Only this afternoon at Mgbidi someone told me that he was from Owerri. I asked whether all was well, he said all was well.'

'Did you expect him to tell you that all was not well and risk being branded a saboteur?' I said. 'Owerri has fallen. The landlord's uncle has returned.'

'No, it can't be true,' my husband insisted.

'It is true. What next? Where do we go from here? Owerri is only twenty six or twenty seven miles from here. We have to think of another place to go to. We are not safe here.'

My husband and brother could not eat that night, especially as the landlord confirmed the news when he returned from Orlu. But he was still optimistic. That was the guiding spirit, optimism. Everybody in Biafra was optimistic. Whatever happened, Biafra was going to win in the end. She was going to win not because she had superior weapons but because her cause was just and God was on her side.

'Never mind,' the landlord told us. 'The Vandals would be wiped out in a matter of hours. Owerri people will soon go back to Owerri. You have gone back to Ugwuta.'

'Yes, but Ugwuta is battleground,' I said.

'Yes, but you and your husband did not see the Vandals there when you went there.'

I lacked his optimism. It was not easy for me to be optimistic knowing what was happening. I was merely deceiving myself if I thought that all was well. All was not well.

The following morning, Kal came. He was in army uniform. He was a major. Kal had enlisted in the army.

'Bravo Kal,' I said when I saw him. He came in a commandeered car. Kal had his own car which he had hidden somewhere and used somebody else's. That was Biafra. Those who were in and out of the State House, who had access to Ojukwu preserved their cars, and used those commandeered from transporters and traders and business-men. Served all of us right. We all were collectively responsible. We all must pay collectively for our folly.

He was full of himself as usual. How come that he had enlisted so soon after the fall of Ugwuta? He now had a batman, a nephew of his who was in school at the outbreak of hostilities. He too was in uniform. When was he trained? And Kal, when was Kal trained? His shoulders showed that he was a major. Wonders would never cease. Kal, a major. A lot could happen in a short week. Anything was possible in Biafra.

We didn't ask him when he left Ugwuta. My brother saw him that morning driving out of Ugwuta. That was before the first warning rocket. Thank God for that warning rocket.

Kal brought us some stockfish and tinned foods. Trust Kal to remember his less fortunate friends in a time like this.

80

'I told you I would join the army if Ugwuta was invaded,' he said triumphantly.

'That is great,' my brother said.

'Tell us Kal, how did we wipe away the Vandals from Ugwuta?' Chudi asked.

'Very simple. It was a mad invasion. It was a suicide bid. To be quite frank, they should not have invaded us. The gallant Biafran forces were at the other side of the Lake. The young officer who was there simply refused to withdraw his men when he saw the Nigerian troops land. He was only a first lieutenant. He said he was going to shoot any of his men who attempted to desert. So that when we attacked from our side of the Lake, they also attacked from their side of the Lake. You see.'

Kal was talking as if he had led the attack himself. He couldn't fire a gun.

'So in a matter of hours the Vandals were wiped out,' Kal continued.

'How?' I asked.

'Very simple. We attacked them when they least expected it. We did not give them time to dig in. There was only one route, that was by the Lake. There was no other way of escape. In the middle of the Lake, their gun-boat sank.'

'The Woman of the Lake sank it,' I said.

Kal laughed. 'Yes, that's what our women said when I spoke to them at Mgbidi. They did not believe that the boats were all hit by artillery fire. Uhamiri saw to the destruction of the Vandals.'

'Are you going to Ugwuta then?' I asked.

'It is not safe yet. It was a battleground only four days ago. I'd rather wait if I were you.'

'And you, aren't you going to Ugwuta? I mean after all it should have been cleared?'

'No. I must fight now. People like us should enlist now to save Biafra. I am committed to saving Biafra.' Kal said.

'Kal, you haven't told us what really happened. Who organised the attack?'

'Ojukwu himself,' Kal said. 'And don't call me Kal, I am Major Kal now.'

Nobody spoke for sometime. So it was true that he organised the attack.

'And some mercenaries?' my brother asked.

'No, there were no mercenaries. We have no mercenaries. He was lying. He was no longer Kal. He was a Biafran officer now. He was Major Kal.

Kal was in a hurry. He dismissed as rumour the news that Owgerri had been taken by the Federal troops. He spoke of a Brigade attack that night. He was leading it. When did he learn how to shoot?

It was left for us to decide what to do. Left to me, I was not going to stay in Akatta. I was going to a place where I would not hear the sound of a gun. I was tired of taking cover. My nerves were shattered.

My husband and brother arranged for another visit to Ugwuta. When they got there, my brother's house was virtually empty. The barn in our house was empty. There was not a single yam in it. My brother's car had disappeared. He had hidden the four wheels and tyres in the ceiling. Someone had broken open the ceiling taken the wheels and tyres, fitted them on to the car and driven away. My brother wondered where the looter got a battery because he carried away his own battery. It was all because the people had refused to sell petrol. His car had been stolen because he had no petrol to drive it.

The more courageous ones had returned to Ugwuta, many more had gone to the farm. The farm was the saviour of the people. In the farm life was hard, but the time was harvest time, and if even one did not plant, one was sure to have relatives who planted and harvested. Perhaps we would go to the farm. Better to wait for the end of the war in the farm.

The end? Could there be an end to this ping-pong
Secretly, I had hoped that the invasion of Ugwuta was
to be the end of the war. I had hoped that the Nige
would hold it and thus end the war. Holding Ugwuta
no flights to Uli airstrip, which meant no arms a1
ammunition. Now we had contained them, now w
wiped them out and the war had continued. The wa
nearly came to an end.

What next? Owerri, if it had not fallen by then, was
siege. Was it wise to return to Ugwuta? If the Nigerians
another attempt to invade Ugwuta by water, and they
same time pushed on to Uli airstrip what were we in Ugwuta
going to do? We would all be brutally slaughtered. No, it was
not safe to go to Ugwuta. But then what next? Remain in
Akatta?

No, we must go back to Ugwuta. We just had to go back. If
there was no food, the Lake was there, and there were fish in
the Lake. So we told our parents that we were going back to
Ugwuta.

At first they did not approve. Later, they consented,
having seen that there was nothing they could do to stop us
from going.

In the morning we got our things ready. My husband and
brother went to Orlu to buy petrol. There they saw the
refugees from Owerri streaming in, old and young, rich and
poor, goats and chickens. The line was endless. Owerri had
fallen to the Federal troops. The people of Owerri were
angry and bitter. They complained that the arms and
ammunition reserve for the defence of Owerri were used for
the defence of Ugwuta. As a result, when the Federal troops
struck, there was nothing left with which to defend Owerri.

At Orlu that morning, my husband and my brother saw
many Ugwuta people who had not heard of the good news.
They rejoiced on hearing the news and got ready to go back
to their home. The fact that Owerri had fallen did not matter

to them at all. Their home had been rid of the Vandals. That was all that mattered to them.

Back from Orlu, we got ready to go home. We thanked the landlord and his family and drove away. In less than an hour, we were at Ugwuta once again.

The place was desolate. How long did the Nigerian troops occupy the town? Nearly forty hours. There was no life. No goats, no chickens, nothing. Everywhere one went, one saw clear evidence of battle. A battle that did not last longer than ten hours. The thatch-houses overlooking the Lake were all burnt down. There was evidence of mass graves beside the burnt down houses. The barns were empty. Bullet holes gaped from the walls of the houses that were still standing.

The only thing that stood undisturbed, unmolested, dignified and solid was the Lake. The Lake owned by the great Woman of the Lake. If defied war. It was calm, pure, peaceful and ageless. It sparkled in the sunlight, turning now blue, now green as the sun shone on it.

My husband and I stood gazing at it. Far in the distance was the gun-boat, sunk as the people thought not by artillery fire but by the Woman of the Lake. She in her depth sank it with her huge fan, for daring to disturb her peace with her people. She sank it for daring to carry war to her own beloved people.

Uhamiri heard the pleadings of her people. She did not turn a deaf ear. She heard them. And she had acted according to the belief of the people. No invader coming by water had ever succeeded in Ugwuta. Uhamiri was the people's hope and strength. Uhamiri be praised.

What was to be done about the pollution? The great Lake had been desecrated beyond description and imagination. Bodies of dead soldiers were floating on the Lake. The gunboat had sunk very near the Urashi River. Poor soldiers.

They could have escaped. They had just a few hurdles more. They could have made it. They nearly made it.

Many people were not home yet. There was no home to return to. They had to wait until the end of the war to start rebuilding. They would rebuild. If they were alive when the war came to an end, they would pick up again from the ruins of war.

We turned our back to the Lake, and made for home. On our way home we met women, middle aged women in white. There was a little boy who dragged an unwilling white ram behind them. They were Uhamiri worshippers. They were going to the shrine of the Great Spirit to sacrifice to her for delivering them from the furies of the Vandals.